Rhett in Love

NEW YORK TIMES BESTSELLING AUTHOR

J.S. COOPER

Formatting by Inkstain Interior Book Designing
www.inkstainformatting.com

Thank you to David Berkeley for giving me permission to use lyrics from his songs in my book. Also for writing the song, "Clementine" specifically for Rhett in Love.
All song lyrics displayed in this book are written and owned by David Berkeley (Straw Man Publishing) © All Rights Reserved.
"Back to Blue" by David Berkeley - *The Fire In My Head*. Straw Man Publishing, 2013.
"George Square" by David Berkeley - *Some Kind of Cure*. Straw Man Publishing, 2011.
"Fire Sign" by David Berkeley - *After The Wrecking Ships*.
Straw Man Publishing, 2003.
"A Moon Song" by David Berkeley - *The Confluence*. Straw Man Publishing, 2001.
"Homesick" by David Berkeley – *Some Kind of Cure*. Straw Man Publishing, 2011.
"Shelter" by David Berkeley- *The Fire in My Head*. Straw Man Publishing, 2013.
"Clementine" by David Berkeley- Written for J.S. Cooper's *Rhett in Love*. Straw Man Publishing, 2014.

For more information on David Berkeley, you can visit his website here:
http://www.davidberkeley.com/

You can listen to "Clementine" on my blog.

DEAR READER,

Rhett in Love is more than just a book. This is more than just a reading experience. There are two parts to this book. Part I is a traditional story and Part II is a story combined with images, music, and videos that provides a fuller experience to the love that Rhett and Clementine share.

I hope you enjoy this unique interactive book.

If you have any issues with Part II, please email me at jscooperauthor@gmail.com.

Lots of love,
J. S. Cooper

ACKNOWLEDGEMENTS

This book would not have been made possible without the following people: David Berkeley, thanks for writing amazing songs. Hollis Chambers, thank you for being such a handsome and kind man, thank you for the videos. Louisa Maggio, the wonderful cover designer. Emma Mack, my editor that works at all hours. Cara Webb, Tiana Croy, Cilicia White, Emily Kirkpatrick, Lisa Petty, Tracie Ridgeway, Stacy Hahn, Chanteal Justice, Tanya Skaggs, and Katrina Jaekley for all your help perfecting the final book.

As always, thanks be to God for all of his blessings. I hope everyone enjoys Rhett in Love.

All good things one day begin.
If l knew the words I'd sing,
I'd sing it loud so we could hear.
We have only this one chance.
Let's take it my dear. Let's taste it my dear.

"BACK TO BLUE" BY DAVID BERKELEY—*THE FIRE IN MY HEAD*

PART I

Prologue

RHETT

Falling in love is just the beginning. It's awesome and amazing, but they're not the only things you feel when you're in love. Love is so much more complicated than I ever thought it would be. Not that I ever really thought about it. I love Clementine O'Hara more than I thought I could love anyone, but that doesn't mean it's easy. Being in a relationship isn't easy. Being in a relationship with your best friend is even harder. My name's Rhett and I never thought I'd be in this situation. I was a certified man-whore. I had fun, women loved me, and there were no complications. Now my life has completely changed and I'm not even sure I recognize who I am anymore. And that's not a bad thing. It's just different. Very, very different. Cos here's the thing - yes, I love Clementine, but that doesn't mean I'm not still the same guy. I'm still Rhett Madison and I'm still a badass. That's something that's never going to change.

 *One*

RHETT

"You can kiss my ass, Rhett Madison." Clementine shouted at me as she slammed the bathroom door. The whole wall seemed to shake for a few seconds afterwards.

"Anytime you wish." I rolled my eyes and walked out of our already messy bedroom and into the even messier living room. "Can't even find a spot to sit down." I groaned under my breath as I pushed Clementine's books to the ground. I stared at them for a second before leaving them there; I knew that my throwing her books on the ground was going to be an issue as well, but I just didn't care. She shouldn't have left them on the couch if she didn't expect them to end up on the floor. "That'll teach you to throw out my Playboy magazine."

Clementine and I had only been dating for a couple of weeks before we moved to Boston together. We'd only been living together in Boston for two months, but already the romance of cohabitation was wearing thin and we were starting to get on each other's nerves. We'd been best friends for over ten years, but being in a relationship was different from just being friends.

"What did you say to me?" She walked out of the bedroom, her face covered in what looked like mud.

"Sorry, who are you and what happened to my girlfriend?" I raised an eyebrow at her.

"What? Oh." She giggled and touched her face lightly. "It's a mask."

"Uh huh." I shuddered.

"It helps to take the impurities out of my pores."

"Uh huh."

"It's good to prevent acne." She continued.

"You don't have to tell me all your secrets, Clementine." I groaned. "Really and truly you don't."

"So I shouldn't tell you about the hot guy that..." She started, but I cut her off by jumping up and lifting her off of the floor and carrying her into the bedroom and dropping her on the bed. "Rhett, my mask is on the sheets." She gasped as she looked up at me with wide brown eyes.

"I don't care." I grinned and collapsed on the bed next to her. "I don't have time to talk about the sheets when I'm busy trying to do something else."

"Rhett, is that all I am to you? A sex toy?" She mumbled and smiled slightly. I saw a small crack in the mask next to her lips and smiled.

"What do you think, Clementine O'Hara?" I grinned at her as she stared up at me with happy joking eyes. Her face looked like she was a monster with the green mask on, and I shook my head. "I certainly didn't sign up for a sex toy that looks like she's just seen a ghost in the middle of a wet and muddy field."

"Don't!" She giggled. "You're making me laugh. I can't laugh or it will crack my mask."

"That's the least of your problems, Clemmie." I looked down at her and gave her a quick kiss, and wiped my lips quickly as I tasted the mud. "What has my life come to? I'm kissing a monster."

"A monster of your making." She groaned as she wiggled against me.

"How is this my fault?" I pinned her arms back. "I never made you go and run around in the mud. And now I come to think of it, what mud is green?"

"Rhett?" She giggled and pushed me away from her and we both started laughing. "Forget about the mud, Jake called me today." She muttered, lines and cracks appearing all over her face now.

"Oh yeah?" I lay back on the bed. "How is he?"

"He's fine. He's loving living on campus."

"I bet, all those freshmen girls looking to have some fun."

"Rhett." She made a face and I held my hands up.

"Not that I want any freshman girls, of course. I only want you. Beautiful wonderful you."

"You're full of crap." She rolled her eyes at me and I groaned.

"How have I gone from being the bees knees to full of crap already?"

"Since I found out you never do the dishes."

"What?" I sat up, my mouth dropping open. "I'm always doing the dishes. In fact, I think I'm the only one that ever loads and unloads the dishwasher."

"You have to turn it on before you unload it Rhett." She shook her head. "It doesn't just wash automatically."

"I assumed you were running it." I shrugged, suddenly feeling bad. Now I understood why the dishes always looked dirty when I unpacked the machine. I'd thought it was because the machine was old, but now I realized it was because the dishes were never being cleaned in the first place.

"Rhett, how would I know to turn the dishwasher on? You're the one that loads it. I assume you're turning it on when you load it."

"So why didn't you tell me before now?"

"I don't know." She looked away.

"Clemmie?"

"Well, everything's been going so well. I didn't want to start an argument after only being here a couple of weeks."

"It's not a big deal, Clemmie." I bit my lower lip. "But seeing as we are telling each other stuff now, there's something I need to ask you."

"What's that?" She paused. "And no, I'm not giving you a blowjob right now."

"Darn it." I winked at her. "That wasn't my question, though. Perfect southern gentlemen don't ask for blowjobs, they receive them."

"You're not a perfect southern gentleman." She laughed. "I don't know who's been lying to you."

"I'm trying to tell you something." I said seriously and she frowned, her brown eyes looking at me curiously.

"What is it?" She studied my face for a second and I had to turn away to stop myself from laughing at her mud-caked face with all the lines.

"You drop your clothes all over the place." I began and she wrinkled her nose creating another crack line in the middle of her nose-bridge.

"What?" She began confused.

"You drop your clothes all over the place." I began again. "On the floor in the bathroom, the living room, the bedroom. I think I even found a bra in the kitchen the other day."

"That's because you undid it when I was making dinner." She shook her head at me and laughed. "You're the one that pulled my top off and then my bra."

"Shh." I laughed and she rolled her eyes as my hand dropped onto her shoulder.

"Oh no you don't." She took a step back as I pulled her towards me.

"Oh yes, I do." I grinned as my lips fell to hers, this time I was able to ignore the muddy taste.

"Rhett." She mumbled and pushed me away. "Let me wash this mask off first."

"I won't say no to that." I grinned and watched as she jumped off of the bed and walked into the bathroom. "And if you want to pick some of the clothes up that you have on the floor as well, before you come back, that'd be great."

"Asshole." She said and I laughed.

"You weren't saying that last night."

"I'll be saying that a lot tonight though." She stood at the bathroom door, her face clean and dripping with water. "And tomorrow night."

"Wow, my girlfriend is back." I jumped up and walked over to the bathroom. "And she looks normal again."

"Whatever." She rolled her eyes and gave me a small smile.

"Yup, she's back to normal." I kissed her lightly on the lips. "And she's looking as beautiful as ever, now that she's not dressed up like a monster."

"Rhett." She groaned. "I need to study."

"Study for what? Finals aren't for months yet."

"Everyone at Harvard studies every day."

"I'm sure glad I don't go there then." I made a face. "And I'm sure glad that I decided to just finish my classes online and graduate from SC instead of transferring to Boston College." I wiped my forehead. "I'll be done in December."

"You know you could never be anything other than a Gamecock." Clementine laughed. "I know you love me, but asking you to graduate as a Yankee would have been too much to ask."

"You got that right." I winked at her. "Ain't no Madison ever traveled out of the South to go to college. No Ma'am. Not before. Not now. Not ever."

"Not ever?" Clementine raised an eyebrow at me. "What about if we have kids and—"

"Clementine." I shuddered and placed my finger on her lips. "You know I love you more than life itself and you know I love sex, but it is way too early to be bringing up kids."

"Rhett Madison." She brushed past me into the bedroom and shook her head. "You're a dumbass."

"Just don't be trying to trap my dumbass self with a kid."

"Excuse me?" Her voice rose and I realized that I'd crossed the line. Suddenly my little joke of humor was no longer funny. I didn't even need to see her face to know I shouldn't have mentioned her trying to trap me. I knew she would take it the wrong way. Just like all women. You made a silly little joke and they always get bent out of shape. Even Clementine and she's about as perfect a woman as I know. However, even Clementine took things too seriously sometimes.

"I was joking Clemmie." I gave her my award winning smile and batted my eyelashes at her. I knew Clementine loved my big blue eyes and I was hoping that they would distract her from being mad.

"You got a fly in your eye, boy?" She frowned at me.

"No." I shook my head and smiled again.

"Good because I'd hate to kill a fly when I slap you." She stood there with her hands on her hips and then pointed her finger at me. "How dare you accuse me of trying to trap you! If you think that I'm the sort of person that—"

"Watches trashy TV?" I interrupted her. "Yes I do think you're that person."

"What are you talking about?" She frowned in confusion at my change of subject.

"You watch those trashy shows and get ideas in your head." I held back a grin. "How do I know you haven't watched one of those Real Housewives shows and decided to trap me with a baby?"

"Rhett?" Her eyes narrowed and her voice grew lower, but I just couldn't help myself.

"They should rename that show Devious Housewives." I couldn't stop myself from laughing. "Or Devious Girlfriends That Want to be Wives."

"You're an idiot."

"Wouldn't you watch that show though?" I grabbed her hand and played with her fingers.

"No." She replied huffily.

"You wouldn't be calling me into the living room to see how someone on the show got pregnant to trap her man after she found out he was cheating on her with her maid or assistant or something?"

"Maybe." She said finally and then started laughing. "Okay fine, it sounds like a show I'd enjoying watching, but I certainly don't want to be compared to one of the women from the show. You'd be so lucky to have a baby with me."

"I was just joking Clementine." My stomach churned as I looked into her annoyed eyes. "You don't really want a baby do you?" My life flashed before my eyes as I thought about us having a baby and all the extra mess we'd have to deal with. It was something I wasn't ready for, plus I knew Nanna would be upset and Clementine's parents would kill me. They hadn't even been happy that we were going to be living together. It was only because Nanna had convinced them that it was better for the both of us. And we'd been friends for so many years and spent so many nights together anyway, that what difference did it make? She'd told them we'd end up spending most nights together in Boston so we might as well live together. It had been my idea of course, but Clementine had been equally as excited. In fact, the day we'd moved in had been the most exciting of my life. Surreal, but exciting. Much like every other day since then had been.

"Rhett, you know I don't want a baby. And who knows, maybe I won't even have a baby with you when the time comes for me to have a baby." She gave me a look and turned around and my heart started thudding. What was she talking about?

"What are you talking about, Clementine?" I frowned and grabbed her around the waist.

"I'm saying don't worry, there are other men that would love to be my baby's father."

"What other men?" I growled down into her face.

"Men you don't know." She licked her lips slowly. "Men that would—"

"Clementine, there are no other men for you." I kissed her hard. "And that's not even—"

"It was just a joke, Rhett." She pulled back and smiled sweetly and rubbed my cheek.

"What?" I frowned, my heartbeat slowing down. "That wasn't funny."

"Just like your joke wasn't funny." She smiled and I shook my head.

"Touché."

"Rhett, you need to calm down." She squeezed my hands. "This is new for both of us. We've been best friends for years and neither one of us knew it would become a relationship. There are still going to be days that we annoy each other and that's fine. It doesn't mean anything. It doesn't mean that I'm going to look for a new man or that you're going to look for a new girl. It's just how relationships go."

"You better not go finding a new man." I took a deep breath as a feeling of fear hit me. I felt like I'd been slapped in the face. I'd never considered Clementine leaving me to be with anyone else. It had never crossed my mind. Yes, she was beautiful and yes other men were interested in her, but it had never crossed my mind that she would give them a chance. So why then, was she bringing it up? Was she considering dating someone else? I frowned as my heart dropped. What if Clementine was done with me, already? Maybe my jokes weren't as funny now that we were dating.

"Rhett?" She frowned as she looked at me, concern in her eyes.

"Yeah, I'm fine." I laughed and she leaned forward to kiss me, her eyes full of love. I ran my hands down her back and grinned. Who was I kidding? Of course, Clementine would never leave me. We were made for each other and I was Rhett. I was the man that every girl wanted to be with. And Clementine had been lucky enough to catch me. There was no way she'd even look at another guy. No way at all. I tried to ignore the voice in the back of my head that reminded me that I still checked out other girls. It wasn't like I was looking to hook up, but how could I not check out the goods?

CLEMENTINE

All good things one day begin.
If I knew the words I'd sing,
I'd sing it loud so we could hear.
We have only this one chance. Let's take it my dear.
Let's taste it my dear.

"BACK TO BLUE" BY DAVID BERKELEY—*THE FIRE IN MY HEAD*

Rhett's blue eyes looked confused as he held me in his arms. I touched his shoulder softly to let him know that we were good. I decided not to tell him that I'd had a scare last week. I didn't think it was the right time. No, I don't want a baby right now, Rhett, but last week I thought there was a chance it had happened anyway. That would go down real well. I hid a smile as I imagined how shocked and scared Rhett would look. He'd be like a big baby himself. There was no way I could deal with two babies right now. And I knew he'd be mad at me. I was the one that hadn't gone and gotten the pill and I was the one that had asked him to enter me without a condom on. I bit down on my lower lip. I'd been stupid. Even though he hadn't come inside of me, I knew the risks.

"What are you thinking about?" Rhett asked me softly.

"I'm thinking that this is an all too serious moment, right now."

"So what do you want to do?" He batted his eyelashes at me and I laughed. I'd never seen a guy that was so cocky and self-assured. Only my Rhett would think he could bat his eyelashes and get sex.

"Isn't that something girls are meant to do?" I said and then giggled.

"Huh?"

"Bat their eyelashes when they want sex." I teased him. "And just in case you got the wrong idea, no we're not about to have sex."

"Why not?" He pouted.

"Because I have homework and we need to tidy up."

"Well, we don't have to tidy up..." His voice trailed off and I wanted to burst out laughing. Rhett was in such denial about the mess in the apartment. He was constantly blaming me for being a slob, but most of the mess was his. He was under the mistaken impression that he was some sort of clean freak because his place back home had always been clean, but that had only been because he had a maid that tidied up behind him.

"Excuse me Rhett Madison?"

"It's your clothes everywhere." He shrugged and gave me a look.

"Rhett, my clothes are everywhere because you pull them off of me, because you want to have sex everywhere." I rolled my eyes at him. "Do you really think I'm disrobing and changing in the kitchen?"

"Your bra was on top of the fridge the other day."

"Because you came behind me when I was cooking." My voice rose and I laughed. "You're in some serious denial. You know that right, Rhett?"

"Who me?" He shook his head. "I think not." His lips turned up in a grin and he paused. "Well, now that you come to explain it a bit, I guess I can see some of your points."

"Uh huh."

"I just thought you'd be a bit tidier Clementine O'Hara." He flashed his teeth. "Considering you're a young Southern lady, I thought you'd know how to keep house a bit better."

"What?" My jaw dropped open at his words. "Are you joking right now?"

"Bad time to joke?" He winked at me and I wrinkled my nose at him.

"Rhett, go and do something. I need to study." I looked at my watch and sighed. "Holden is coming over tonight."

"Hole who?" He froze and his eyes became alert.

"Holden, my assignment partner." I said slowly and looked away. "I told you about him, remember?"

"Noooo," he drawled. "I've never heard about him before in my life."

"You most probably weren't paying attention to me."

"I don't remember you mentioning him." He shook his head.

"Remember I told you, his brother went to school with David Berkeley."

"Who the fuck is David now?" He frowned at me. "Another guy you want to study with?"

"Rhett?" I sighed. "David Berkeley, my favorite singer, remember?"

"Hmmm." He shrugged and looked sheepish. "Oh yeah."

"So Holden is coming over tonight so we can work on our assignment, so I need to get ready."

"Get ready?" He raised an eyebrow and his jaw dropped. "Did you put a facemask on to get your skin all glowy for him?"

"Rhett." I shook my head. "Don't be an idiot. I meant get ready for our discussion, not dressing up."

"Am I going to have to let this guy know what's up?"

"No, we're just friends." I sighed and blushed. I didn't tell Rhett that Holden was hot, really hot. And smart. I knew Rhett wouldn't appreciate hearing about that. Even though he knew I loved him. Even though he knew he was my world. It was funny, I never would have thought that even gorgeous guys could be insecure, but they were as insecure as the rest of us. It still amazed me that Rhett and I were dating and that we'd gone from best friends to boyfriend and girlfriend with very few hiccups. Not that I wasn't worried of course. A part of me was scared that everything would go down badly and I'd lose my best friend and my boyfriend. A part of me was scared that someone like Rhett couldn't change. I mean, how many players went from multiple women to one girl? Not many, I was sure. And Rhett was gorgeous, so all he had to do was go out to have women hitting on him. It was hard dating someone with such good looks and charisma. Though I trusted him. I had to trust him.

"Are you mad at me?" Rhett sighed as he studied my face and I just gazed at him.

"No, I just get worried sometimes."

"Worried about what?" He asked softly.

"If we made a mistake." I looked down. "I don't want to lose you Rhett."

"All good things one day begin. If I knew the words I'd sing, I'd sing it loud so we could hear. We have only this one chance. Let's take it my dear. Let's taste it my dear." Rhett sang softly at me and I smiled.

"I love that you don't know David Berkeley's name, but you know his songs. I love Back To Blue."

"Of course I know his songs; you play them all the time." He grabbed my hands. "But it's true, Clemmie. We only have one life, we only have one chance. We couldn't just walk away from what we have without giving it a shot."

"Don't you ever get worried though?"

"Never." His blue eyes became serious. "There is no doubt in my mind that you're the girl for me."

"But you never wanted to fall in love or have a girlfriend or..." I stopped myself from saying get married. I knew that he didn't want to hear the words married or baby right now. I tried to stop myself from giggling at the picture his face would make if I said the words marriage. Not that I didn't want to marry him. Of course I did. However, I knew it was important to take baby steps with Rhett. It had taken him long enough to figure out he had feelings for me, I didn't want to cause him to go backwards. Not when I'd been in love with him for so many years.

"Or what?" I could see him thinking as he stared at me. The blue in his eyes changed from a light sky blue to a more serious azure color.

"Nothing." I said lightly and turned away from him. I could feel my heartbeat skipping, worried that he'd catch on to what I'd been thinking and flip out. I knew Rhett well enough to know that the words wedding and marriage would cause him to have a heart attack, no matter how much he denied it. It would be too much, way too soon.

"Remember when we went to that movie theater and danced and sang that Hansen song?" He grabbed my arm and spun me around.

"How could I forget? The MMMBop song?" I made a face and he laughed.

"Yeah, remember how we were laughing and dancing?" His eyes crinkled as he recalled the spectacle we had made of ourselves.

"Yeah why?"

"We did that because we thought it was fun. We did it because we had no fear of what other people were going to think. We did it because we were together and we just wanted to have a good time." He squeezed my shoulders. "We were each other's rocks. We can do anything together Clemmie. I'm not scared about what could happen to us because I know that there's nothing that could happen that we couldn't get over. We're still best friends first." He grinned. "And that means I can still tease the heck out of you and not worry that you're going to get all silly and girly on me."

"Phew." I laughed. "I thought you wanted to go to Copley Place, that mall downtown, and perform a new dance routine."

"Hell no." He laughed. "My dancing days are behind me."

"We could do some twerking, Nicki Minaj style." I grinned.

"I think I'll keep my anaconda in my pants, thank you for very much." Rhett laughed and winked at me.

"I cannot believe you know the name to her song, or that you even know who she is." My jaw dropped as I stared at him. I felt warm and secure inside. I loved that Rhett could always push my worries aside so easily.

"I'm dating you. I know all the crappy musicians now."

"She's not crappy." I rolled my eyes. "At least some of her songs aren't crappy." I conceded.

"I don't mind if you want to practice your twerking though." He pulled me towards him and squeezed my ass. "Preferably on my lap."

"You're disgusting Rhett." I hit him in the arm. "I'm not about to twerk on your lap."

"You weren't complaining last night." He licked his lips and playfully slapped my ass.

"Is everything about sex with you?"

"Is that even a question Clementine O'Hara? We've been best friends for years and that was never an issue, do you really think that's all I want now?"

"I don't know what to—"

"Seriously Clementine?" He cut me off and stepped back and his lips quivered. "Is that what you think of me?" I saw his eyes widen and he bit his lower lip. "Do you really think I'm capable of being that sort of man?" His eyes looked dolefully into mine and I burst into laughter.

"You're such a goof." I shook my head after my laughter subsided. "What am I going to do with you, Rhett Madison?"

"I'm going to plead the fifth as I'm not sure you'll appreciate my answer." He grinned and then winked at me again. "However, I can make it easy for you."

"Make what easy for me?" I frowned as I watched him pulling his shirt off. I stared at his bare chest and tried not to burn my eyes out staring at his abs. I didn't understand abs. How did they even exist? How did a stomach go from fat to a well-defined and chiseled piece of art? I ran my fingers down his six-pack and licked my lips. "You wish."

"You do too."

"Rhett, I already told you, Holden is coming over and we're going to study."

"I don't know Holden and I don't care about Holden. What sort of name is Holden anyway?"

"Rhett." I frowned at him and ran to my phone when I heard it beeping. "I think that might be him."

"He's here already?"

"Yes." I read my text messages. "Please be nice."

"I'm always nice." He looked at me with a surly expression. "Why wouldn't I be nice to Holdy?"

"Holden." I rolled my eyes.

"At least he's holding and not grabbing."

"Rhett!"

"I'd have to give him a beat down if he tried to grab you." He cocked his head. "In fact I'd have to give him a beat down if he tried to hold you as well."

"Will you behave?"

"Do you love me?" He asked me softly as I hurried around the apartment and grabbed every item that didn't belong on the ground and threw it into our bedroom.

"What?" I paused as I grabbed up a pair of his boots and ran past him.

"Do you love me?" He stopped me from moving.

"You know I do."

"Good." He smiled and nodded. "That's all I wanted to hear."

"You're crazy, you know that right?"

"I'm crazy in love with you." He whispered in my ear and my heart started thudding. How many years had I waited to hear someone say that to me? Not even I could have imagined that my Rhett would have finally grown up and fallen in love with me. I'd never believed that fairytales could come true before. "Never forget that." He said quietly.

"I'll never forget that." I looked into his eyes. "You know that right?"

His eyes continued to stare into mine and I saw that lost look that sometimes took over his face. The look that told me that even though he was here with me, he wasn't really here. He was thinking about something. He was in another place. A place where he was young, lost, scared Rhett. A place where all his bravado and charisma, was gone. It was a place I'd seen him in many times before, but it was a place we never spoke about.

"Be a good girl or I'll spank you." He joked finally and looked away. "You better go and let Holden in or he'll start to wonder what's going on."

"I'm sure he's already wondering that." I laughed and kissed Rhett quickly on the lips. "Don't mess the apartment up while I go down and get him."

"Don't be too long or I'll send a search party down." He called after me as I ran to the front door so that I could go downstairs to let Holden into the apartment building. I smiled to myself as I made my way down and tried to remind myself that I needed to speak to Rhett later about what was bothering him because something was obviously bothering him. I wasn't sure if he was having cold feet about us. It was a weird situation that we were in, going from best friends to lovers and living together in such a short time. I felt like we'd never really gotten to experience what it was like to just date, without the pressure. We'd moved in together so quickly. We'd gone from Rhett and Clementine, best friends to Rhett and Clementine, serious boyfriend and girlfriend. There had been no in-between.

"Hey Holden, sorry about the delay."

"No worries." He grinned at me as I let him in. "I thought I had the wrong building for a minute."

"No sorry, my boyfriend had clothes everywhere and I was just trying to tidy up before you came up."

"Oh you didn't have to tidy up for me." He flashed his perfect white teeth at me. "I don't mind a bit of a mess."

"Oh I couldn't have you coming over to a mess."

"I guess it's the Southern girl in you." He laughed. "Most girls in Boston don't care." He winked at me and I could see that his green eyes were laughing. I stared at him and tried not to ogle him. Holden looked like a young Ben Affleck and I couldn't stop myself from admiring his serious, studious expression. He was so unlike the guys I'd known back home.

"That could be it. Come on up. I'm sure Rhett's wondering what's taking so long."

"And Rhett is your young man?"

"He's my boyfriend yes." I nodded as we walked up the stairs. "We were best friends for years and just recently started dating."

"Really?" He seemed surprised. "And you guys are living together already?"

"Well, I know it seems fast, but we—"

"What seems fast?" Rhett stood at the front door and surveyed Holden as we walked into the apartment.

"Holden this is Rhett, Rhett, this is Holden."

"I'm her boyfriend, Rhett." Rhett held his hand out and his blue eyes narrowed as he took in Holden's appearance. A part of me thought it was funny that he was acting so possessive and the other part of me was annoyed.

"Holden, her new friend." Holden turned to me and gave me a smile. "At least, I hope you consider me a friend."

"Of course I do." I beamed at him. "You're my first friend in Boston and at Harvard. It's not easy being the new girl; especially being from the South."

"What's wrong with being from the South?" Rhett frowned.

"There's nothing wrong with being from the South." Holden said diplomatically. "I think there's just an idea of what people are like who are from the South. Good ol' boys and all that."

"Good ol' boys?" Rhett gave me a look and then turned back to Holden. "What does that mean?"

"Well you know." Holden continued uncomfortably and I wanted to tell him to stop while he was ahead. "I think there are three sorts of people from the South: the rednecks or cowboys or whatever, the plantation folk that wish slavery was still around to pick their cotton and tobacco and the migrants from the North that wanted a slower pace of life."

"Really now?" Rhett drawled. "I guess you just know your Southern boys well, huh? We're all into Nascar, Country Clubs and going on about the good ol' days."

"Well, no." Holden's face turned red. "I didn't mean to stereotype or say that was all that exists. I'm sure everyone doesn't love Nascar and every guy isn't into pickup trucks."

"Rhett loves pickup trucks." I grinned and punched Rhett in the shoulder. "And stop picking on Holden. He's going to think we're unfriendly."

"No offense about pickup trucks." Holden made a small face and Rhett rolled his eyes at me. I knew exactly what he was thinking, just from his expression. He thought Holden was an idiot. He thought Holden was a wimp and everything he disliked about guys from the North. Holden unknowingly was proving Rhett's thoughts about how Northerners thought about Southerners and I knew that Rhett was going to let me know exactly what he thought as soon as Holden left.

"No offense taken." Rhett muttered. "I don't say nothing about you damn—"

"Rhett, why don't you go and watch TV in the bedroom." I glared at him to shut him up before he said something we'd both regret.

"I'll go and call Tomas. You know he's coming up tomorrow." Rhett reminded me and then looked at Holden. "And yes, Tomas is a Hispanic fellow and there's no need to be shocked. We are allowed to have friends of other races now."

"Rhett." I growled at him and he laughed as he sauntered to the bedroom. "Sorry about that."

"It's okay." Holden looked a bit unsure of himself. "I hope I didn't offend him."

"Don't worry; it takes a lot to offend Rhett. He was just joking with you." I smiled at him, trying to let him know that everything was cool. "The truth is there are many older folks that do wish that we were back in the 30s and 40s, but me and Rhett, we're not plantation kids. Well, I'm not at least. I don't come from old money and I don't come from a family that thought those days were better."

"I didn't mean to insinuate that you guys were—"

"Ooh insinuate, such a big word. I guess he's a Harvard guy." Rhett mumbled out loud so both of us could hear. I knew he was doing it to make Holden uncomfortable and I shook my head.

"Excuse me please." I walked to the bedroom and closed the door behind me. "Stop it, you're being rude."

"Who me?" Rhett looked at me with wide eyes. "I didn't mean to be."

"Yes, you did."

"I didn't." He gave me a small smile and I sighed.

"You're insufferable Rhett. You know I need to study."

"You're always studying." He sat on the bed. "I hope you will be able to hang out with Tomas and me tomorrow."

"Tomorrow?" I bit my lower lip and tried not to sigh. I knew he wasn't going to like my answer.

"Yes, tomorrow." His eyes narrowed.

"Well, Holden and I are meeting up again tomorrow to finish our project."

"But you're meeting now?" He looked upset.

"We're starting it today and finishing it tomorrow."

"What?" He sighed and lay back on the bed. "Fine."

"I'm sorry. I'll make it up to you."

"Yeah you will." He rolled over and winked at me. "You'll make it up to me alright, for about an hour and thirty minutes as soon as he's gone."

"Rhett." I could feel my face growing warm as he licked his lips and winked at me. There was something so special about our connection. All he had to do was look at me in a certain way and I felt my body warming up.

"That's my name." He grinned. "I'll have you screaming it out by the end of the night."

Three

RHETT

"Dude, let's go to a strip-club." Tomas grinned as he walked out of the bathroom, his hair slicked back and wet.

"I can't go to a strip-club." I shook my head and laughed. Tomas was one of those guys that would never change.

"Don't tell me, Clementine's taken your balls and cut them off." Tomas raised an eyebrow at me and looked around the living room.

"What's that supposed to mean?"

"Dude, you've always been down to go to see some big ol' titties bouncing in your face, why can't you go now?"

"You know why not." I frowned, as I started to feel irritated at Tomas, and he'd only just arrived.

"Because you have a girlfriend." He said in a singsong voice. "Where is she anyway?" He plopped down on the couch. "This living room looks like a hot mess. Doesn't Clemmie like to tidy up?"

"Dude, I have spoken to her about the living room." I could feel my face heating up.

"And she still hasn't done anything." He pulled a bra out from the chair he was sitting on and threw it at me. "Here you go. Maybe I'll find your panties as well."

"You're a dick." I grabbed her bra and sighed. "She's at some study session with some prick from Harvaarrd."

"Nah, I'm just a guy with a dick." He paused and looked at me. "I think yours is gone."

"So she cut my balls and took my dick?"

"Didn't she?" He raised an eyebrow and then laughed. "Dude, come on, let's go and have some fun. We haven't done shit since I've been here."

"We're going bowling tomorrow." I knew as soon as I said the words that they sounded lame. "And you've only been here for a day."

"Yay." He shook his head and he looked away from me. "We can go bowling and Clementine can go on her study dates."

"Look if you really want to go to a strip-club, we can go to a strip-club." I jumped up, feeling angry that Clementine was with Holden again and grabbed my wallet. "We just got to be back before Clementine gets home."

"Pussy."

"You want to go or not?"

"I'm coming, dude. I'm coming." He jumped up with a huge grin. "Don't let me make you change your mind. Let's go play some real or fake."

"You're a pig." I laughed as we walked out the front door. Real or fake was a game we'd played in South Carolina when we went to the strip club. We'd try and grab girls' boobs and see if they were real or fake. I'd usually feel them up with my hands, but Tomas liked to try and grab them with his mouth - which wasn't always accepted by the strippers. We'd been kicked out of several strip clubs in our time, but it had always been fun.

"So you don't want to play?" He looked disappointed as I turned him down.

"No, I don't want to play." I frowned at him as we left my apartment building and I realized that I wasn't just saying that. I had no interest in touching or seeing other girl's breasts. I didn't even feel excited about the possibility.

"Come on dude, what happened to you?" Tomas frowned. "You know I love Clementine, but you're still in your twenties, you're too young to become some pussy-whipped old man. Is this really the life you saw yourself having after college?"

"Did I see myself dating Clementine and living in Boston? No." I answered. "But then there are a lot of things I didn't see or think about."

"I can't believe you moved here, bro. You messed everything up. I hooked up with Penelope last week and she—"

"You hooked up with Penelope? Clemmie's ex best friend? The girl that tried to fuck me in the back of my truck?"

"Yup." He grinned at me.

"Are you out of your mind? She's crazy!"

"I didn't say she wasn't, but you ever fuck a crazy chick? They are down for basically anything."

"I'm going to be sick." I cringed. "Are you desperate?"

"What?" He frowned. "Where's my high-five? What's up with the judgment? Boys don't judge man. What's Clementine done to you?"

"I'm not judging you man, but you can do better than Penelope."

"All of us don't want a perfect girl like Clementine."

"What's that supposed to mean?" My voice sounded surly and I stopped in the street.

"Are we really going to do this bro?" He frowned. "What's going on with you?"

"Nothing." I sighed and reached out and gave him a quick man hug. "It's good to see your handsome face Don Juan."

"That's racist that is." He grinned.

"It's not racist if it's true." I laughed.

"Why I gotta be Don Juan, why can't I be—" He stopped and burst out laughing at my expression. "Got ya bro, take a chill pill. Life isn't so serious. It's about fun. Love, sex and fun. It seems to me that you've forgotten that."

"The expression is love, sex and rock n' roll." I corrected him and he groaned.

"Let's go see some titties." He pulled out his phone. "Let me Yelp it, I got a feeling you ain't got no idea where the strip-club is."

"You know what, I really don't." I shook my head in surprise. "I don't even know where the local pick-up joints are. I don't even know how freaky girls up here are in bed."

"You think they're freakier?" Tomas eyes lit up.

"You'll have to tell me." I grinned and I felt my stomach curdle. "It feels weird saying that."

"What?" Tomas looked at me in confusion.

"Saying you'll have to tell me. I'm normally the one that's doing the telling."

"You wish, bro." Tomas shook his hair and smiled as two girls walked by. "Have a great evening ladies." They looked at him and giggled and he gave them a huge smile. "I'm only here for a few days, so if you need some Tomas loving, come back on by." He called after them and they giggled and continued walking.

"They looked like they were in high school." I shook my head and he laughed.

"Dude it's only illegal if you touch them. I ain't got time for no high school chicas, you know that. 21 and up, bro. That's all I want." He ran his hands through his hair and grinned. "But that doesn't mean I can't show them what they're missing. I'm a smooth, sexy, love machine."

"I hope I never sounded like that." I groaned as he started gyrating in the street as if he were an extra auditioning for the Magic Mike Two movie.

"Dude, you sounded worse. Hi, I'm Rhett. I'm blond, blue eyes and tan. I look like a regular Ken. I'll pick you up in my mustang and fuck you in my truck, but don't bother calling me 'cos you won't hear from me again. I'll be too busy sucking up to my nerdy best friend Clementine O'Hara. And don't you dare say we're more than friends or I'll rip your head off."

"Asshole." I laughed, knowing that what he said was true. "You want to go to the strip-club or not?"

"I'm looking bro, what do you think 'XXX Girls' or 'A Night in Heaven'?"

"Seriously?" I sighed and then groaned as my phone rang. "Hold on, it's Clementine." I answered the phone quickly. "What's good?"

"What's good?" She drawled lightly, mocking me. "I see Tomas made it there safely."

"Yeah, haha. What's up?"

"I was just calling to see what's going on." She paused. "Does something have to be up for me to call?"

"No. Tomas and I are just about to head out. Are you coming home now?" I asked hopefully.

"No, Holden and I are going to have a late night." She sighed and I could hear some music playing in the background.

"Studying with music?" I said lightly, feeling annoyed thinking about Clementine with that schmuck Holden. There was something about him that irritated me. It might be the simple fact that he was spending one-on-one time with my girl, or it might have been my body telling me that there was something off about him. All I knew was that I felt tense about the fact that they were spending so much time together. I did not trust him. He wanted my Clementine and he was using the guise of studying to get closer to her.

"It's Mozart, Rhett, not Barry White."

"Do you wish it was Barry White?" I said, knowing I sounded jealous. I could see Tomas staring at me with keen eyes.

"Rhett, I gotta go." She said in a tired voice. "I'll see you both later."

"Shall we wait to have dinner with you?"

"No." She said quickly. "I told you, it's going to be a long night. I won't be back 'til late. Eat without me."

"Okay fine."

"What are you guys going to do?"

I know I shouldn't have lied, but really how do you tell someone you're dating that you're going to a strip-club? Maybe it's just me. Maybe it's because I haven't been in a relationship before, but I couldn't tell her. Which was sad because I had always told Clementine before. I had no secrets from her. She knew who I'd been with, when I'd been with them, how I'd met them. She knew everything about me and I'd never been scared to tell her anything before. I knew as soon as I said the words that I was crossing a line that I'd never crossed before. "I think we're going to go bowling."

"Oh that should be fun."

"Yeah, I'm hoping to get all strikes."

"You never get all strikes." She laughed. "I wish I was going as well, I wish I could show you how it's done."

"I'm the one that taught you how to bowl Clemmie."

"Well the student is now better than the master." She giggled and even though her tone was lighter, I didn't feel better.

"In all things?" I asked softly, but she pretended she didn't hear me.

"Have a good time bowling. Tell Tomas I'll see him in the morning and that I'm sorry to miss his first day in Boston."

"I will." I paused. "Have a good time studying, don't do anything I wouldn't do."

"Before or after you dated me?" She asked softly and I felt as if I'd been kicked in the gut. Was she joking or being serious?

"Is that a joke, Clementine? Because if it is, it's in very poor taste."

"Oh Rhett, relax." She sounded annoyed. "I'll see you later." And then she hung up. I stared at the phone in my hand and frowned. I couldn't believe that she'd hung up on me already.

"Trouble in paradise?" Tomas looked concerned.

"Dude, what paradise?" I rolled my eyes. "Clementine has become a different girl now that we're dating."

"That's girls bro. She's got you by the short and curlies and she ain't going to let go."

"Short and curlies?" I shook my head at him. "What is that?"

"I got it from some English show I was watching." He grinned. "Describes your relationship perfectly."

"You decide on a club yet?"

"A club or a bowling alley?" He raised an eyebrow at me. "You lying already bro?"

"Dude, she doesn't want to hear about me going to see naked girls."

"That's why I don't date. I can't deal with these jealous bitches trying to put me on lockdown."

"Not cool, Tomas." I frowned. "Don't call Clementine a bitch."

"What? I didn't call her a bitch."

"Girls aren't bitches, that's not cool."

"Oh shut the fuck up, Rhett." Tomas gave me a look. "You were down with bitches and hoes this time last year, don't go getting all holier than thou on my ass now, just 'cos you've been with this chick for a few months. You're going to be back to the bitches and hoes as soon as you and Clementine break up."

"Excuse me?" My body stilled at his words.

"Not trying to be rude dude, but c'mon. You're both in your early twenties. This is your first relationship and you used to be a player. This is her first anything. The likelihood of you both working out is not high." He shrugged. "I mean she's already spending late nights with some other guy, listening to music."

"You need to stop eavesdropping." I muttered. "And I told you, they're studying."

"Do you think all he cares about is studying?" He laughed. "If it was you, what would you be doing?"

"Huh?"

"If it was the old Rhett 'studying' with a hot girl, would you be just listening to music for no reason?"

"That muthafucka is trying to get into her pants." I exclaimed loudly and Tomas nodded.

"He's most probably got his hand on her back and asking if she wants a massage to help with the stress."

"What stress?"

"The stress of dating a punkass like you." Tomas pulled out a piece of gum and started chewing. "She just hung up on you, so she's obviously frustrated. He's going to see that and try to act all nice so he can get up in there."

"She wouldn't let him do anything." My head was starting to hurt at the thought of Holden trying to make a move. "She loves me."

"You know how many girls love me?" Tomas started gyrating again. "And you know how many girls I love? Love don't mean shit."

"That's not true." I turned to him. "When you talk about love, you're talking about lust fueled love. What Clemmie and I have is different. Our relationship is based on trust, respect, honesty and a deep love."

"That's why you just lied to her?" He said softly and I looked away. We stood there in silence for a few moments and I felt confused. I didn't really understand why I'd lied. I think it was because I didn't want her to be disappointed in me. And I didn't want to give her an excuse to let her guard down with Holden. I just didn't trust him. I felt a hollow feeling inside as I wondered why trusting her wasn't enough.

"WHERE ARE YOU going?" I asked Clementine as she walked past me in her short shorts and t-shirt early the next morning. I groaned as I stared at her through foggy eyes.

"Out." She turned and looked at me. "Is that okay warden?" She smiled quickly and my heart stopped for a second as I thought about her.

"Funny." I rolled my eyes and then rubbed my forehead. "I feel like shit."

"You guys got drunk at the bowling alley?" She looked amused. "Tomas was snoring when I woke up."

"We didn't wake you up when we got in, did we?"

"No." She walked over to the bed and sat down. "I was fast asleep. I was exhausted from all the studying. I'm glad you guys had a good time."

"Yeah, we did. So where are you going now?"

"I'm going to pick up some breakfast and coffee for all of us."

"Oh. Nice." I grabbed her hand and tried to smile, though guilt filled me as I thought about all the naked breasts I'd seen the night before. All breasts and no bowling balls.

"So I better go now before the lines get too long." She bent down, gave me a kiss on the cheek and then stood up.

"Are those shorts appropriate?" I frowned as I stared at her long legs.

"As appropriate as it was for you to go to the strip-club yesterday." She snapped at me, her eyes light as she stared down at me with disappointed eyes.

"I told him not to go." Tomas yelled out from the living room as I stared at Clementine in shock. "It's not appropriate for you to go and get lap dances when you have a girlfriend at home." He continued shouting.

"Tomas." I shouted back angrily. "How did you know?" I asked her quietly, feeling mad at myself.

"First off, you got a lap dance?" Clementine glared at me and my heart sunk.

"Honey." I gave her a quick smile and she just stared at me with her hand on her hip. Oh shit! I thought to myself. I wasn't sure how I was going to get out of this one. "I didn't, I mean I—"

"Oh Rhett." She started laughing loudly. "When will you learn you can't lie to me? Bowling alley my foot."

"I'm sorry." I made a face. "How did you know?"

"Tomas had photos of the two of you all over Facebook last night." She laughed. "I knew the minute you hit the club because he took a photo of the sign. *One Night in Heaven?* Really?"

"Tomas." I shouted back at him. "I'm going to kill you." This time he didn't respond.

"And after you kill him, I'm going to kill you, Rhett Madison."

"For going to the strip-club?"

"No, for lying to me." She sighed. "I mean, I kind of of get why, but I don't like it."

"I didn't have fun."

"He's lying again." Tomas shouted out from the living room. "He had a great time."

"Tomas, shut up." I growled.

"It's fine, Rhett. I know who you are." She sat back down on the bed again. "I just don't want you to lie to me anymore."

"Fine, I went to a strip-club and I had a lap dance."

"One?" She asked softly.

"Two." I sighed.

"He's lying. He had four." Tomas shouted again and I knew that he was two seconds away from feeling my fist in his face.

"I didn't really enjoy them though."

"Now that's true." Tomas said. "He didn't even grab any of their boobs. He didn't even want to play real or fake."

"Well, that's good." Clementine rolled her eyes. "You got four lap dances?" She asked me softly and I could see the hurt in her eyes.

"It didn't mean anything to me." I grabbed her hand. "I only went for Tomas."

"We'll talk about it later." She sighed. "I need to get breakfast and then I have a call with Holden in two hours."

"Another one?" I let go of her hand and turned away from her and closed my eyes. When was this guy just going to go away?

"We're finishing up a project Rhett."

"Yeah, okay. Go and get the coffee, I'll see you later." I mumbled, not knowing why I suddenly felt so bereft inside. There was a coldness seeping in and I wasn't sure why.

"I know you're not mad at me, Rhett Madison." Her voice was annoyed. "Mr. I got four lap dances while I told you I was bowling last night."

"And how was studying?" I finally opened my eyes up and looked at her. "Was that all you did?" I asked accusingly, knowing I was acting like a jealous boyfriend. I had absolutely no reason to think that anything else was happening. I knew I was being irrational and then I saw the red hue rising in her face and my stomach dropped. Maybe I wasn't being so irrational after all.

CLEMENTINE

So I open the window,
hoping the breeze blows.
Birds going crazy.
I'm wondering how they know.

"THE FIRE IN MY HEAD" BY DAVID BERKELEY—*THE FIRE IN MY HEAD*

It's funny. You always think that once you get the guy, everything in your life is going to be great. And if he loves you, well what more can you ask for? That's the dream right? Meet the right guy; fall in love and everything else is smooth sailing. That's not always how it works out. No one told me that going from friends to lovers was going to be so hard or so different. Not one person. Well, asides from Penelope. And I didn't want to hear a word she had to say. I mean, how could I trust her advice? She'd tried to sleep with him. Just thinking about them touching made me cringe.

"I'll have three black coffee's please and three cheese croissants." I smiled at the barista though I really wanted to get Rhett some veggie juice or something. I'd played it off and smiled at his lies, but I was hurt and upset. I didn't understand why he'd lied to me. I mean, I understood that maybe he didn't want me to know about the strip-club, but to keep up the lie was hurtful. It was even more hurtful to know that he'd gotten a lap dance - several in fact. A part of my brain wanted to know exactly what had gone on during the lap dance. Had he gotten hard? Was he attracted to any of the women? Did he wish he could spend the night with any of them?

"Any sugar?" The barista asked me and I could tell this wasn't the first time.

"Sorry, no." I apologized. "I was thinking about something."

"That's fine." She looked bored. "You can go and wait over there."

"Oh okay, sure." I nodded and walked to the end of the counter.

"Clementine?" I heard Holden's voice behind me and turned around.

"Hey," I smiled at him weakly, not wanting to think of the night before.

"I thought that was you. How are you?"

"Fine." I nodded, a bit freaked out. What was he doing here?

"Last night was good. I think we're going to ace the assignment." He smiled at me again, his dimples making his face look more boyishly handsome.

"I hope so." I nodded.

"About last night..." He started and paused. "I just wanted to say sorry."

"It's fine." I nodded awkwardly; as I thought about the light kiss he'd given me on the lips as I'd been sitting on the couch waiting for the pizza to arrive.

"I thought that..." His voice trailed off and we both stood there awkwardly.

"It's okay. No harm, no foul."

"I really like you Clementine." He looked into my eyes searchingly. "I know that maybe I shouldn't be saying this."

"You don't even know me." I shook my head, my voice and eyes pleading with him to stop.

"What I know I like."

"I have a boyfriend."

"He's a meathead." He made a face. "No offense, of course, but I don't know, I don't think he's right for you."

"You don't even know him." I sighed. "Please, don't say anything else. Rhett is my best friend, he's my—"

"You do realize that you just said he's your best friend? You didn't say that he's your boyfriend. You didn't say he was the love of your life."

"Holden." I was getting annoyed. "It doesn't matter what I say, please stop."

"Even though he lied to you?" He sounded confused. "In my book, it's not a very trustworthy boyfriend that tells his girlfriend that he's bowling when he's busy getting a hand job at a strip-club."

"That's not fair." I sighed, wishing I hadn't told him about Rhett's lie. "And he didn't get a hand job."

"Okay then, a blowjob." His face reddened. "I'm sorry to use such crude language with you, but what do you think goes down at strip-clubs?"

"I'm not going to talk about this with you." My face grew warm with humiliation as I thought about Rhett getting a hand job in the strip club. He wouldn't do that, would he? I bit on my lower lip as I tried to remember the stories he'd told me from before we started dating. What had he done before? I knew that he and Tomas used to like to touch the girls' breasts and bet if they were real or not and I knew that he'd once had an accident in his pants when he'd worn only sweatpants and nothing else. I felt sick even thinking about that story, but I knew I couldn't bring it up. It was a story he'd told me when he was 18 and it had only been his second trip. I couldn't allow myself to get jealous over something that had happened in his past.

"So do you want to talk about the assignment now, seeing as we're both still here?" He asked eagerly and I knew that Holden was not going to get the hint.

"I have to take the coffee's and croissants back for Rhett and his friend Tomas." I shook my head. "They are waiting on me. And I don't have my books. We'll talk on the phone later."

"I can come back with you if you want." He asked eagerly. "Maybe we can—"

"Holden, no." I shook my head. "I'll call you later." I sighed.

"Am I coming on too strong?" He made a face.

"It's not that, but you know I have a boyfriend."

"I can wait."

"Wait for what?" I asked stupidly, and immediately regretted it.

"For when you break up." He smiled weakly and my eyes bore into his with what I hoped to be a look of disdain. "Sorry." He followed up quickly. "That was wrong of me."

"Yeah it was." I sighed. Maybe Rhett had been right. Maybe Holden was after more than friendship. And then I started laughing at myself. I could see from Holden's face that he was confused, but I didn't care. There was no maybe about it. Holden was definitely interested in me. And if I was honest, it made me feel kind of good. Though it also made me feel guilty. Was I emotionally cheating on Rhett if I liked the fact that a very handsome and smart guy was interested in me?

"Are you okay, Clementine?" Holden's eyes searched mine. "I'm sorry for being inappropriate. I should have just apologized and left it at that."

"Yes, you should have." I touched his shoulder. "Look Holden, I'm not interested like that, but if you want to stay friends that's fine. Please don't try and kiss me again."

"I can't promise I'm not going to hope for more." He grinned. "That's okay, right?"

"Holden!"

"What?" He laughed. "Stranger things have happened. Do you know how many people meet when someone is dating someone else? A lot, that's how many. I know you don't want to think about that now, but it's just life. This could be how our story starts."

"Holden!" I exclaimed again. "Please don't."

"It's true." He grinned. "There are movies based on love stories like this. We'll look back and laugh at this."

"You're making me uncomfortable." I told him honestly and turned to see if my coffees were ready.

"You're not in South Carolina anymore, Clementine. There's a whole big world out there. A world that exists outside of your friendship with Rhett. From what I've seen—"

"Stop." I held my hand up. "You don't know me and you don't know Rhett. Just stop."

"Just because it's comfortable doesn't mean it's right." He said softly. "You can't stay in a cocoon, just because he's the only one you've ever known."

"You don't know my life, Holden." I said angrily as I grabbed my coffees.

"I know more than you think." He grabbed his coffee and walked outside the store with me. "I dated my high school girlfriend for years. And then we both went to college and we realized that what we had was nothing compared to what we could have."

'That's sad. Everything isn't bigger and better."

"You're better." We stopped outside my building. "I know that and we've never even been on a date."

"How could you possibly know that?" I pulled out my keys.

"I knew it the moment we had our first conversation." He smiled at me gently. "I knew it when I looked into your eyes. As soon as I saw you, I knew you were the one."

"Holden, that's awfully romantic, but I already told you that—"

"It's okay." He smiled at me. "I'm a patient guy. When something's meant to be, it'll be. Love isn't meant to be hard. Love isn't based on lies. Love isn't comfortable. Love just is."

"I'll call you later, Holden." I opened the door quickly and ran inside and then shut it firmly. Was Holden a psychopath? I could feel my heart beating at his words. Why was he saying those things to me? He didn't even know me. Holden had made me very uncomfortable, but he had made me think as well. Was I letting Rhett get away with too much? Had I made it too easy on him? He'd done whatever he wanted whenever he wanted and I'd just been there sitting on the sidelines. And as soon as I'd started dating and he'd realized he was falling for me, I'd become his. I hadn't made it hard on him. Even now, he was doing what he wanted without thinking about me. Did he really love me? Or was I just a possession to him that he didn't want anyone else to have. I walked up the stairs slowly thinking hard. Was this for real? Was he really the one? Had I made things too easy for him? Was he going to tire of me? And if he did, would I lose him forever? Would I even want to be friends with him if he broke my heart? I stopped outside our door and leaned against the wall as I struggled to gain my composure. Everything had moved so quickly and everything wasn't going as smoothly as I'd hoped for. I didn't feel like I was living in the dream I'd always imagined my love story to be. I didn't feel any real romance from Rhett. I didn't feel like he really truly adored me. All he ever seemed to want was sex. He never surprised me with flowers or a homemade meal. He never wrote me poems or letters. He never called to tell me he loved me just because. He never did any of the things I'd always dreamed about having in a relationship and I didn't know how to tell him. I mean how could I expect anything different? He'd never been the guy that was full of romance. He'd never been the guy to sweep a girl off of her feet and I wasn't sure why I'd hoped things would be different between us.

I opened the door slowly and walked into the apartment. Rhett and Tomas were sitting at the dining table glaring at each other and I hoped that we weren't about to revisit the strip-club story.

"Where've you been?" Rhett jumped up and walked over to me, a look of contrition on his face.

"I went to the coffee shop. And Holden was there and we talked for a bit."

"Of course, he was there." He sounded annoyed.

"I didn't know he was going to be there."

"Yeah, sure." He took his coffee and walked to the large navy couch. I walked over to the table and gave Tomas a coffee and a croissant and sat down across from him.

"So how've you been?" I took a sip of coffee and ignored Rhett's glare.

"I hope I didn't start anything?" Tomas looked uncomfortable as he bit into his croissant. "You know I didn't mean any trouble. I just wanted me and my boy to have some fun, like we did in the old days."

"The old days were a couple of months ago." I said in a monotone. "And I didn't stop you, did I?"

"Rhett didn't want to go." Tomas spat out. "I made him. It's my bad."

"He didn't have to go if he didn't want to. I assume you didn't have a gun to his head?"

"Well no."

"And I assume you didn't force those four women to give him lap dances?" I raised an eyebrow at him and he made a face and looked at Rhett. "It's fine Tomas. I know you're just trying to be a good friend. Rhett and I will discuss it later."

"Well, you guys can discuss it now." Tomas jumped up quickly. "One of the girls from last night just text me and she wants to show me some new moves."

"One of the strippers?" I asked in disbelief. He wasn't seriously going to go and hook up with a stripper, was he?

"Hell yeah." He jumped up. "I need a shower, and then I'm out. I'll catch you both for dinner later?"

"Sure." My jaw dropped as he ran into the shower and then I looked at Rhett. "Is he being serious?"

"He sure is." Rhett nodded, a small smile on his face.

"Did you ever hook up with a stripper?"

"Never." He said solemnly. "I've never done anything with a stripper, well asides from that time I was wearing the sweatpants and you know."

"Yes, I know." I cringed. "No need to remind me."

"That's a mistake I'll never make again." He grinned.

"What's that?" I asked softly.

"I'll never get a lap dance in sweat pants and no underwear. I swear it felt like she was rubbing on my cock directly." His face froze as he realized what he'd just said. "Shit, I guess I fucked up again huh?"

"No." I stood up and walked over to the couch and joined him. "You didn't fuck up because you told me a story I already knew, Rhett."

"But I can tell from your face you're not exactly impressed." He rubbed my shoulder.

"I don't want to think about you exploding in your pants and coming because some dirty stripper was rubbing up on you, Rhett." I shook my head and rolled my eyes. "Would you want to hear about me dirty dancing with some guy and having an orgasm and no panties on?"

"What the fuck?" His eyes narrowed and his breathing grew heavier. "That did not happen, did it?"

"Would you want to hear about it if it did?" I sat back in the couch, quite enjoying the look of jealousy in his eyes.

"Hell no." He frowned. "Did this happen? And when and with who?"

"Rhett." I snuggled into his chest. "You know everything about me. Have I ever told you a story like that before? Am I the sort of girl that goes out with no panties on?"

"I'd like you to be." He kissed the top of my head and I could tell that his breathing had calmed. "But yeah, no, you've never done anything crazy like that before."

"But if I had you wouldn't want to hear it right?"

"No, I wouldn't want to hear it."

"It's the same with me. I don't want to think about you with other girls, Rhett."

"I'm sorry." He grabbed my hands. "I'm just so used to telling you everything."

"I know. This is a hard transition for both of us."

"I never thought it would be so crazy." He shook his head. "I thought it would be so easy. We've been together forever, but this, this is so different."

"I know." I nodded. "I don't want it to be different. I don't want us to be different. I don't want us to hide things from each other."

"I'm sorry for lying about the strip-club." He made a face. "I really didn't want to go, but then I figured I might as well."

"Did you enjoy it?" I asked him softly.

"Do I have to answer that?" His blue eyes glittered.

"No." I huffed out, starting to feel jealous myself.

"Would you believe me if I told you I didn't enjoy it?" His fingers ran across my cheek and he nipped at my nose. "Would you believe me if I told you that all I could think about was you and what you were doing with Holden." He growled. "I'm sorry for being jealous, but that guy gives me the creeps."

"So, there's something you should know." I paused as his eyes become alert.

"Uh huh and that is?"

"So, maybe Holden tried to kiss me and maybe he thinks he wants to date me."

"What?" He glared at me. "When you say he tried to kiss you, what exactly did he do?"

"His lips lightly pressed against mine." I whispered.

"You kissed him?" Rhett jumped off of the couch at the same moment that Tomas came back into the room.

"Uh, is this a bad time?" He cracked a joke and we both glared at him.

"I didn't kiss him." I jumped up. "He kissed me and I pulled away from him."

"And you still went to meet up with him this morning? What the hell, Clemmie?"

"I didn't go to meet up with him. He happened to be there at the same time."

"Yeah right."

"I didn't kiss him back and I told him off." I muttered. "It's not like I'm into him."

"He knows you have a boyfriend, why did he kiss you?" Rhett grumbled, still looking pissed.

"He said that he doesn't think you're good enough for me." I said, my face turning red.

"Oh snap." Tomas exclaimed and then headed to the door. "I think I'mma head out right now."

"Yeah, that sounds like a good idea." Rhett's eyes never left mine. "Call me when you're headed back."

"Most probably tomorrow." Tomas said and opened the door. "I'll see you two lovers later."

"So do you agree with him?" Rhett asked as soon as Tomas closed the door.

"Agree with who?" I said softly.

"Do you agree with butt face? Do you think I'm not good enough for you?"

"Are you joking Rhett Madison?" I took a deep breath. "If I agreed with him, would I still be here? Would I have told you?" I pressed my fingers into his chest. "You're really annoying me, you know that right?"

"I'm annoying you?" He pushed a finger into my shoulder.

"Yes." I stuck my tongue out at him.

"You're annoying me." He stepped towards me and leaned down. "And that tongue is mine." He whispered before taking it into his mouth and sucking on it. His lips pressed down on mine and my hands reached for his hair as we kissed deeply and passionately. I felt his hands on my back running down to my hips and bringing me towards him. My breasts crushed against his chest and he groaned against my lips as his right hand moved up to the back of my head. I kissed him back eagerly and slipped my hands down the back of his boxer shorts and touched his tight ass. "Don't play with fire, Clemmie." He groaned and adjusted his position so that his hardness was pressed up against my stomach. "I want you so badly."

"I know." I laughed and touched his hardness tenderly. "Your body's telling me that."

"Your fingers are telling me that that makes you happy." His hand grasped my fingers. "Can we make love or do you have something to do?" There was a hopeful look in his eyes and a thrill of excitement ran through me as I stared into his bright blue eyes.

"I think there's something we could do that would be pretty exciting."

"Oh yeah?" He leaned back and looked at me as his hand ran up to my breast. "What's that?"

"Well, I was thinking we could go out and—"

"I don't want to go out." He looked disappointed.

"Listen to me, Rhett." I grinned. "We can go out somewhere and you know."

"No." He shook his head. "What?"

"You know." I blushed as I waited for him to get it. He was so slow sometimes.

"I know a lot of things, but I have no idea what you want us to go out and do, unless it's me going over to Holden's and giving him a piece of my mind."

"Forget Holden. This is about us." I squeezed his hardness again and he groaned.

"Clemmie..." He muttered as he played with my nipple.

"Rhett, I want to go out without any panties."

"No panties?" He looked intrigued and then it hit him. "Oh, no panties." His eyes lit up. "Are you saying what I think you're saying?"

"Yes." I nodded shyly, unable to believe what I was agreeing to. "Let's go and get it on outside of the house."

"Yes!" He picked me up and swung me around the room, carrying me to the bedroom and dropping me on the bed and then collapsing next to me and kissing me all over.

"Rhett," I pushed him off of me. "If you keep this up we won't make it out of the house."

"So where are we going?" He asked excitedly. "A restaurant? I've always wanted to have sex in a booth."

"Are you joking?" I laughed. "How obvious would that be?"

"You'd just get on my lap and pretend to be whispering something to me."

"That's not going to happen." I laughed. "There is no way that people would not suspect that we're having sex."

"How's about in the movie theater?"

"No Rhett."

"At the gym?"

"How are we going to have sex at the gym?" I rolled my eyes at him.

"Well, you can go on the—"

"Not happening Rhett." I giggled. "I was thinking a restroom at the mall."

"What?" He made a face. "A restroom?"

"You know, one of those family restrooms." I stroked his face. "We could rush in and then do it and sneak back out again."

"Oh." He stared at my lips. "That's not exactly what I was thinking?"

"What were you thinking?"

"Something a bit sexier, a bit kinkier."

"Rhett." I groaned. "How kinky?"

"Well not public restroom kinky." He laughed.

"I don't know. I don't want anyone to see us."

"Isn't that part of the fun?"

"You think people watching us would be fun?" My jaw dropped. Did Rhett have a thing for people watching him have sex? How had I never realized that before?

"No silly." He ran his hand up the side of my thigh. "The thrill is the possibility of getting caught. Getting caught itself is not fun, trust me."

"You've been caught before?" I asked softly, my heart pounding.

"No, but Tomas has." He grinned. "And let's just say his grandma and her friends weren't impressed."

"His grandma and her friends?" My eyes widened. Had Tomas slept with one of his grandma's friends?

"Yeah, he went to visit her at her retirement home and hooked up with one of the nurses." He laughed. "He wasn't invited back, I can tell you that."

"Tomas is such a dog." I shook my head. "I can't believe some of the stories you tell me about him."

"He hooked up with Penelope." Rhett said hesitantly and I knew he was scared that he'd get into trouble for bringing her up.

"No way, what?" I gasped, unable to believe my ears. Penelope had been one of my best friends until recently. Our friendship had faded after I'd found out she'd tried to sleep with Rhett. I could have forgiven her for that fact as she'd attempted to have sex with him before I'd been dating him, but even after she realized we had feelings for each other, she tried to manipulate the both of us and I couldn't forgive her for that.

"Yup. She's such a ho."

"Rhett, that's not nice." I shook my head and frowned. "Why is she the ho? Why isn't Tomas a ho?"

"They're both hoes." His fingers slipped under my shirt and made their way up to my bra.

"Then do you think you're a ho as well?"

"I'm a one woman man now, Clemmie. I'm no ho."

"Why are we talking about ho's?" I moaned as he unclasped my bra.

"I have no idea. There are other things I'd rather be doing." He leaned down and kissed my stomach. "You taste like peaches." He licked up to my breasts and pulled my top up.

"Rhett." I moaned. "Be quiet." I grabbed his head and pulled him down to kiss me.

"Wait, no." He paused a mere inch away from my lips.

"What?" I groaned, wanting to feel him against me. My body was crying out for his touch. It was like he was made for me and me for him. When we made love, I felt as if my whole body were on fire. There was nothing that connected us more than the physical act of sex and I couldn't quite get over how amazing it felt.

"What about the park?" He whispered before nibbling on my left nipple.

"The park?" I squirmed on the bed, wishing I hadn't brought up the public sex idea. It had been a spur of the moment thought and now it seemed that Rhett didn't want to let it go.

"Not a bench or anything." He laughed. "We'll take a picnic and then we'll take a nap together."

"A nap?" I was confused.

"Well, we will pretend we're napping." He grinned and then winked at me. "Capisce?"

"I think so." I could feel myself getting excited. "You think it will work?"

"I know so." I could see he was excited as well. "Come on, let's go."

"Wait, I have to change my shorts to a skirt." I giggled as I tried to do my bra up again.

"No, no, take that off as well." He laughed. "No bra and no panties."

"Rhett." I groaned. "You're a pervert and you're corrupting me."

"Don't you like being corrupted?"

"No." I laughed as I pulled my top off and then took my bra completely off. I could see Rhett's eyes narrow as he stared at my naked breasts. I stared at the throb in his throat and smiled sweetly.

"What are you thinking?" I asked softly as I walked to the closet and looked for another top slowly.

"I'm thinking we might not make the park." He walked up behind me and kissed my shoulders as his hands circled my waist and then reached up to cup and squeeze my breasts. "God, but I love you Clementine." He groaned in my ear as he pinched my nipples, his erection pressed into my ass. "Only you can make me feel like this." I closed my eyes as he fondled my breasts and kissed my hair. "I love the smell of you. I love the touch of you. I love the taste of you." He whispered into my ear as he kissed it. "Let's never argue again. Let's only be together, happy and carefree."

"Life doesn't always go like that." I moaned as his fingers touched me more aggressively.

"We'll beat life at its' own game, my love." His right hand slid down between my legs. "Now let's go have some fun in the park."

RHETT

We were back in George Square when the rain gave way.
There's something in how the spring comes so suddenly.
And the dress she wore was yellow.
And the rain was in her hair.
How bad I wanted to tell her that I would always be there.

"GEORGE SQUARE" BY DAVID BERKELEY—*SOME KIND OF CURE*

"But we don't actually have a picnic." Clementine looked around nervously as we placed the sheet on the ground.

"We have a picnic basket that looks like we had a picnic and an old wine bottle."

"It just seems so devious." She groaned and held her skirt tightly to her legs.

"The wind isn't going to blow your skirt up Clemmie. You're not going to be exposed to the world."

"You have no idea what could happen." She blushed and then groaned. "This is seeming like a really bad idea, Rhett."

"Why?" I pulled my belt off and placed it in a plastic bag. Then I looked down and realized that had been for nothing. I wasn't going to be taking my pants off, so I really didn't need to take my belt off.

"I can see little kids." She moaned and ran her hands across her eyes. "Let's not and say we did."

"Let's do and say we did." I said and then grinned and looked around. "What kids are you talking about? I don't see anyone."

"I just saw a little boy riding past on his bike." She made a face.

"Clementine, we're covered by a bunch of trees. I really doubt that anyone is going to see us."

"There are eyes everywhere."

"Yeah, I mean maybe someone has a pair of binoculars and is spying on us, but they're not going to see much, we'll be under the blanket."

"Binoculars? What?" She made a face and I groaned. Now I was giving her reasons to say no that she hadn't thought of.

"I mean I doubt anyone has any." I said stiffly and grabbed her hands. "Come on, Clemmie, this is going to be fun. Just some good ol' fashioned American fun."

"Sex in the park is good ol' fashioned American fun?" She raised an eyebrow at me. "Really? Did the President create a law that said all ye citizens must have sex in public places."

"Yes, he did." I laughed. "He even said that those going for citizenship can prove their loyalty to the country by engaging as well."

"That's a great exam to have to pass." She paused. "First, tell me if you can name the first President of the United States and now tell me if you've had sex on a park bench?"

"I have heard that there have been no complaints." I nodded as I kissed her lightly. "All new citizens have been polled and they love their new country."

"Hmm," she kissed me back. "Does that mean that I'm going to be kicked out if I say no."

"Yes, Clementine. If you do not have sex with me in the park today, you'll be sent packing back to the country of your forefathers."

"What country is that then Rhett?"

"Where's Nanna from again?"

"You mean her grandparents?" She laughed. "Nanna is American."

"Shhh, whoever." I said and then sucked on her lower lip and my hand ran up her back. "It doesn't really matter."

"Well, they say that all people originate from one lady in Africa." Her breath was low as my fingers moved forward and brushed her breasts.

"Africa?" I paused and looked into her eyes. "Nanna's from Africa?"

"Nanna's not from Africa and her parents aren't from Africa. However, all of humanity is from Africa, back in the very old days when the first people were made."

"Adam and Eve are African?" I stood back and blinked. "I sure didn't know that. Who told you that?"

"No one told me that." She rolled her eyes. "And I have no idea if Adam and Eve were African. I'm just telling you what anthropologists say based on the oldest remains they've found."

"So wait a minute, if we're all descended from this one lady in Africa does that mean we're related?" I joked and shuddered. "Does this mean that what we're doing is so very wrong on another level?"

"You're sick, Rhett." She punched me in the arm and then squealed as I pinched her nipples. "That's not even something funny to joke about."

"What incest isn't cool?" I leaned forward and ran my tongue across her lips.

"Rhett, you know how to kill a mood." She mumbled and I grinned at her.

"And I know how to bring it right back again." I pulled her down to the ground with me and pulled the blanket over us before moving the back of her yellow dress up.

"You're not just going to go for it, are you?" She moaned as my fingers touched her wetness. Her legs tightened on my hand and I kissed the back of her head as I rubbed her clit.

"I'm not going to go for it unless you want me to."

"Rhett, we can't do this." She rubbed her ass back into me.

"Would you rather we talk about the beginning of the world or spies instead?"

"Neither, Rhett. I don't want to talk about..." She cried out as I slipped a finger inside of her. Her pussy walls clenched on my finger and I could feel her heart racing as I fingered her. I growled into her hair as I played with her and she whimpered.

"Does it feel good?" I asked gently as I pulled my fingers out of her.

"You tease." She moaned and turned over to face me. "You know that it feels great." Her eyes were full of lust as she reached down and unzipped me. "I can't believe you're corrupting me again, Rhett Madison."

"Corrupting you or making you a woman." I gazed into her light brown eyes and pulled her face to mine. "Whichever one it is, I'm glad for it."

"All those nights you shared my bed, you really wanted to be doing this." She giggled and I shook my head as I turned her and mumbled into her shoulder. All of a sudden, I felt serious inside. "I don't want you to think that. I wasn't secretly hoping to make love to you every time I slept in your bed."

"Oh no?" Her fingers were soft and cold on my semi-hard cock and I closed my eyes as she moved her fingers back and forth quickly.

"Clementine." I groaned as she squeezed the tip and I felt my cock growing in her hands. "You've got a magic touch."

"Shhh." She moaned as I played with her breasts.

"I just can't wait anymore." I groaned and turned her back to the other side so that we were spooning. I moved in closer to her and positioned myself between her legs. My cock was now completely hard and it slid next to her pussy effortlessly. I could feel her juices as I teased her clit and she moaned.

"Please Rhett." She muttered as she gyrated back against me.

"Fuck it." I mumbled as I played with her breasts. "I forgot the condoms."

"No." She sighed. "Just no."

"And you didn't get on the pill and not tell me, did you?"

"You know I'm not on the pill yet." She cried, while still gyrating back against me.

"I'll pull out." I placed the tip of my cock at her entrance and rubbed against it. "I'll pull out when I think I'm going to come."

"Okay." She groaned and backed up into me as I slid my cock inside of her and held onto her hips. "Ooh, Rhett. Oh." She cried out as I moved in and out of her. Her pussy felt so wet and tight and I felt myself drowning in her body as we moved together as one. The trees surrounding us made me feel like we were at one with nature. I felt primal and protective and high. Clementine's skin felt so silky and smooth as my fingers ran up and down her body. Everything about the moment was perfect, asides from the fact that I knew I was close to coming. We'd been fooling around for much of the day and I hadn't had a release and I knew that I was ready to blow my load soon.

"You feel so good, Clemmie." I groaned into her ear as I fucked her hard. I tried to concentrate on making her orgasm first and not on how badly I wanted to come.

"Fuck me harder Rhett." She cried out as I slowed my pace down.

"I can't go faster right now." I grunted as I paused. "Give me a second." I mumbled as she clenched her pussy on my cock. "Please Clementine, I don't know if I can—"

"Rhett." She cried out and before I knew it, she had pushed me back on the ground and was on top of me, riding me hard. Her hair was flying in the wind in abandon and her yellow dress clung to her body as she moved back and forth on me. "Oh yes," She screamed as she reached down and kissed me, never once stopping her movements up and down. I groaned as she rode me hard and I felt the lightest drops of rain on my face.

"Clementine," I grunted and held her hips, but she was lost in her own world as she moved back and forth on me. I felt my load exploding inside of her and she screamed as she started to orgasm as well.

"Rhett." She screamed as she collapsed down on top of me, her face wet from the rain and sweat. "Oh Rhett." She kissed me hard as she rolled over to the side.

"Oh Clementine." I grabbed her face and gazed into her eyes. "You're so fucking hot."

"We should leave soon." She ran her hands down my chest. "It's raining and I need you again."

"I need you again as well." I laughed and caressed her face, before pausing. "You know I just came inside of you right?"

"I know." She nodded. "I got carried away, I wasn't even thinking about that."

"We should be fine." I kissed her lightly. "But we have to be more careful next time."

"I know." She moaned. "I never thought I could be so irresponsible."

"None of us are—"

"What's going on here?" A loud male voice shouted behind me and we both froze. I turned over slowly, praying to God that it wasn't who I thought it was. My heart sunk when I saw the police officer.

"Hi officer, my girlfriend and I were just waking up from a nap." I nodded at him and I knew that Clementine was freaking out.

"You came to Danehy Park to sleep?" He gave me an incredulous look.

"Yes officer. Well we had a picnic and then fell asleep."

"And sleeping involves screaming? Or did you both have nightmares?"

"I, uh…" My voice trailed off as I fiddled with my zipper. I turned to look at Clementine and her face was bright red as she avoided eye contact with me. "Well, it's raining now officer, so I think we're going to head home."

"I don't think so young man." He stepped towards us. "Both of you get up and don't make any sudden moves."

"Sudden moves?" I asked and he frowned. "Really officer, we'll be fine. We were just saying we're ready to go home."

"I'm sure you were." He pursed his lips. "However, I'm about to change those plans. I think you'll be enjoy a trip to the precinct."

"Precinct?" My heart stopped. Clementine was going to kill me. She was literally going to rip my heart out and eat it with her bare hands.

"I'm going to have to take you both in for sex in a public place and indecent exposure."

"What indecent exposure?" I jumped up. "We're both dressed."

"Young man, are you threatening me?" He grabbed his baton.

"What?" I asked incredulously. Was this guy crazy?

"Do not raise your voice at me." He said in a deep tone and I knew that I had to be careful with what I said next.

"Officer, I want to apologize for our actions today." Clementine jumped up and said softly. "We were irresponsible and we have learned our lesson. Please don't arrest us." I saw the police officer staring at Clementine for a few seconds and I could see that he was taken in by her.

"If you just let us go, I can give you a thousand dollars." I spoke up and I heard Clementine groan. I knew immediately that I'd fucked up.

"Are you trying to bribe a police officer sir?"

"Please, officer." Clementine stepped forward. "My boyfriend and I are new here, we're from South Carolina and well life's a bit different there. Please forgive him, he's just confused and worried. I promise you that if you let us go, you won't see us here again."

"Lady," the officer addressed her with a frown. "I'm going to let you both go with a warning, but I want to give you some advice. Find a better boyfriend. A guy that loves you would be taking you out for a nice dinner and to a nice hotel for some real loving. This piece of cheap scum is only looking out for himself. He's what we call a player. Any guy that is taking you to the park to get romantic is not the guy for you. Trust me, I'm a good judge of character. I know men like him. You seem like a nice girl and I think it'd serve you well to listen to my advice."

"Thank you, officer." Clementine nodded and I froze feeling furious. How dare he try and tell my girlfriend to leave me? He was obviously looking for a beat down, but I knew that if I laid one finger on him I'd be going away for a long time. I sighed and looked to the ground. "Rhett, help me gather up this stuff." Clementine hissed at me, with fire in her eyes. "And let's go."

"I'm going to leave you all to it now." The officer stared at me with narrowed eyes. "I expect you both to be out of the park within five minutes."

"Yes officer, thank you officer." Clementine nodded and grabbed up the sheets and stuffed them into the bag. "Let's go Rhett." She handed me the empty picnic basket and we walked quickly towards the exit in silence. We made it to the street before I turned to her.

"So is this my fault?" I looked at her to see if I was going to be the one getting the blame for her being loud and riding me.

"It's not my fault." She glared at me. "Mr. let's pretend we're having a picnic and have sex in the park."

"You're the one that said, ooh take me somewhere naughty and fuck me."

"I never said that." She said angrily.

"Oh, just like you said, I'm not going to wear any panties?" I shook my head. "I guess I made you say that as well."

"I said that." She stopped and sighed. "Fine, fine, fine. I thought it was going to be fun. I didn't think we would get busted by the police."

"So you didn't have fun when you came?" I asked her softly and watched her blushing. "Was that just a figment of my imagination, Clementine?"

"Whatever." She gasped as I bit down on her lower lip hard and sucked.

"I had fun when I burst my load inside of you." I pulled away and whispered in her ear and she looked at me in shock.

"You're a pig, Rhett. A real pig."

"I'm just being honest." I shrugged. "That was fucking hot how you pushed me on my back so you could fuck my brains out."

"Rhett." She groaned and started walking again.

"Am I lying or not?" I started walking again, knowing I was digging myself into a deeper hole, but not knowing how to stop myself. "That was the hottest sex I've ever had."

"Fine Rhett. Am I supposed to feel proud of that?" She muttered. "My male slut boyfriend thinks I'm his hottest lay."

"I didn't say you were the hottest lay, I said you were the hottest sex." I muttered angrily and then realized what I'd said. "Not that you're not also the hottest lay as well. You're the most beautiful woman I've—"

"Shut up." She turned to me, her eyes furious. "If you want to make it out of this alive, you need to shut up."

"You're mad at me?" My jaw dropped. "What did I do?"

"Oh grow up, Rhett. It's not always about you, just grow up."

"Wow, no need to be a bitch." I mumbled.

"What did you just call me?" Her voice rose as we walked up the steps to the front door of our building.

"I didn't call you anything." I was annoyed. When had Clementine made the move from understanding, loving and sweet Clemmie to the shrew I now had to deal with? What was her problem? A part of me was wondering if we'd made a mistake in deciding to date. Our whole relationship had changed. Some days I felt like it was just as I remembered it, but other days I got so annoyed and frustrated with her. And she just didn't seem to understand where I was coming from.

"You called me a bitch." She said through clenched teeth. "I'm the bitch because you convinced me to have sex in the park?"

"I never said you were a bitch and it didn't look like you needed much convincing to me." I shrugged. "When you pushed me back on the ground and sat on my cock, that was all you. When you screamed out my name and rode me like some cowgirl from Texas, that was all you."

"Whatever Rhett, if you can't have a civilized conversation about this." She shook her head as we walked up the steps.

"Civilized conversation about what?" I opened the front door. "You're the one that is making this a bigger deal than it was."

"You're the one that made me have sex in the park. We nearly got arrested Rhett. That could have been on our records for life."

"Are you being serious?" I dropped the picnic basket on the floor. "This is all my fault?" I took a deep breath. "Is this because I went to the strip-club? Are you still mad at me? Is this your way of expressing your hurt because I got a couple of lap dances? Or is this because I titty fucked Penelope? Or is this because I've had sex before with other women? Are you jealous because I've been with other people? Is this your way of taking it out on me?"

"What?" Her jaw dropped and she threw the bag with the sheets to the corner before walking up to me. "Are you fucking kidding me?"

"Okay." My heart sunk at the expression on her face. "So maybe that wasn't it then." I gave her a weak smile. "I love you, Clementine." I whispered, but she didn't smile back.

"You think I'm upset because you had a past before we started dating?" She poked her finger into my chest. "You think I'm jealous because I'm upset we nearly got arrested and you offered to bribe the officer."

"So maybe I was wrong." I grabbed her hand. "For trying to bribe the police officer and for saying you were jealous."

"You think?" She glared at me for a few seconds, her brown eyes angry.

"I was very wrong. I'm sorry jellybean."

"Don't call me jellybean." She made a face, but I could see she was softening.

"You look pretty in your yellow dress." I tried again.

"Like a jellybean?" She cracked a smile and I felt the stiffness in my back loosening as I realized she was no longer mad.

"No, like the sun." I grinned.

"Uh huh."

"I'm sorry." I made a face. "I messed up."

"It's fine. I messed up as well." She sighed. "I think that—"

"You look so sexy." I stepped forward as I interrupted her and kissed her. "Are you ready for round two?"

"Rhett!" She groaned as my fingers pulled her dress up and off. She stood there naked in front of me and my heart pounded as I stared at her.

"You're so beautiful Clementine." I touched her delicate skin softly.

"We should talk Rhett."

"We can talk later." I shook my head and pulled my shirt off.

"We can't just..." Her voice trailed off as I took my pants and boxers off and stood there in front of her naked.

"I want to make sweet love to you, Clemmie." I stepped forward and grabbed her hand and placed it on my already hard cock. "I'm so turned on right now."

"Rhett." Her eyes were uncertain as she played with my cock. I grabbed her other hand and pulled her down to the rug. "Ooh, Rhett." She groaned as I spread her legs and buried my face in her pussy, my tongue licking her up eagerly, loving the taste of her on my face.

"Shh, we can talk later." I lifted my head up and gave her a quick smile, before burying my face back in her wetness and sticking my tongue inside of her. She cried out and I felt her inner thighs clenching my face as I ate her out. I smiled as I felt her body trembling underneath me and sucked down on her clit. I was good at sex. I knew that. I knew that I could make her come. I knew that

I could make it all better with sex. As I felt her juices pouring down on my face, a thought flashed through my mind. A thought that made me think twice about what I was doing. A thought that made me worried and scared. We were having make-up sex, but we hadn't really addressed any of the problems that we had in the relationship. And there were definite problems that were showing up already. Problems I didn't know how to fix. Problems that we hadn't had as best friends. Problems I was scared could end the relationship. I closed my eyes so that I could focus on making Clementine feel good, but I knew that hot sex wasn't going to seal the cracks that were already developing between us. I was scared inside. I was more scared than I'd ever been in my life. I loved this woman more than anything in my life, but I didn't know if that was going to be enough.

CLEMENTINE

And all that we've been through
Don't leave me
I won't leave you
And all that we've been through
Be with me
I'll shelter you

"SHELTER" BY DAVID BERKELEY—*THE FIRE IN MY HEAD*

"I'll miss you guys." Tomas gave me a quick hug before turning to Rhett. "Y'all have to come back home soon."

"Yeah, we're going to come for Thanksgiving and Christmas." Rhett spoke up and I could feel my stomach churning. What was he talking about? I hadn't been planning on going home for Thanksgiving as I had to study for finals.

"Okay great." Tomas grabbed his bag. "I can't wait. I better go as the taxi's waiting for me."

"Have a great flight back, Tomas." I smiled at him. "I enjoyed having you here. Give Jake a big hug for me and tell him he needs to get his ass up here soon."

"Will do, Clemmie." He rubbed the top of my head. "Thanks for having me guys."

"Bye." Rhett gave him a slap on the shoulder. "Stay safe, bro."

"You too." Tomas walked out of the door, flashed another smile and left.

"I'll miss his crazy ass." Rhett said after closing the door.

"I'm just glad he's not here to take you to strip-clubs every weekend." I smiled at him and he laughed in response. We both stood there for a few seconds awkwardly and I sighed. "We should talk." I bit my lower lip nervously. I didn't want to have this conversation. At all.

"Yeah." He nodded and looked at me with a sad face. His expression made my heart stop and I walked to the couch.

"So," I started, but my voice cracked and I didn't know what to say.

"So," He said and we sat down on the couch.

"About the other day." I took a deep breath. "I want to apologize."

"What happened the other day?" He frowned.

"The day we were in the park." I smiled. "I shouldn't have blamed you for us getting caught or for us having sex in the park. I think I was just stressed and worried and still in shock."

"It's okay." He nodded. "I understand Clemmie. And I should apologize as well. I'm the one that convinced you that the park would be safe."

"You'd try and convince me of any and everything, Rhett." I laughed and stared at him. "You've got a way with words."

"Well you know." He grinned and winked at me.

"But after that, when we were arguing, we said some things." I frowned. "I think we should talk about them."

"Talk about what?" He frowned.

"Just what's going on between us?" I made a face. "I know this isn't what either one of us was expecting."

"What do you mean?" His expression changed and he looked worried.

"You know what I mean, Rhett." I sighed. "I know you stop yourself from telling me stuff now. I know that this is different for both of us."

"Are you breaking up with me?"

"No." I shook my head. "But I'm scared Rhett. Everything was so easy between us and now, well now..." My voice trailed off and we just stared at each other.

"No one said it would be this hard, did they?" He half-laughed. "I don't know why it's this hard. I don't know what I'm doing wrong. Maybe I'm not cut out for relationships."

"Rhett, I think both of us need to adjust our expectations of what this relationship should be like."

"I'm not the boyfriend you've always dreamed of having, am I?" He looked sad. "I wish I was that guy, but I have a past, Clemmie."

"It has nothing to do with your past, Rhett." I shook my head. "I knew about your past. I just expected a bit more romance."

"What do you mean?"

"I mean romance, not just sex." I looked at his confused expression. "I know that you might not understand. I just don't know how to explain this to you." I mumbled. How could I tell him that I thought he used sex to solve everything? How could I tell him that I felt like he wasn't truly giving himself to me? How could I tell him that I wanted him to woo me, and that I wanted to feel his deep devotion on a daily basis. How could I tell him that I didn't feel like his girlfriend, but more like his best friend with benefits? I was scared to tell him. I was scared that he would respond badly. I didn't know how he would respond because he'd never been in a real relationship before. I knew that he wasn't emotionally equipped for conversations like this and I didn't know how to approach the topic.

"I booked us for a class." He spoke up and grabbed my hands, his blue eyes light and unsure.

"What?" I frowned. "What class?"

"A relationship class." He gave me a half-smile. "Don't look so shocked." He stroked my face. "I saw it in the newspaper the other day. I thought it could help us."

"So you've been worried about us as well?" I felt hurt, though I knew I was being irrational.

"I've been worried that you're going to leave me." He looked away. "I know that I use sex to make things better and I know that at the end of the day, sex is not going to be enough. I know you need more from me than I'm currently giving. I don't want you to leave me, Clementine."

"I'm not going to leave you, Rhett." I reached out and grabbed his face. "Why would I leave you?"

"That's what happens in life." He shrugged. "People leave when things get rough." His eyes looked into mine and I could see the pain reflected in his expression. It was a pain I'd seen shining through from his soul for many, many years.

"I'm not going to leave you, Rhett. I'm not your mom." I said softly and my heart broke for the man sitting in front of me.

"We don't know what's going to happen." He shrugged. "I just don't want to give you a reason to leave or stop loving me." He muttered and as I looked into his face I was taken back to his thirteenth birthday party. And the empty look of sadness that had been on his face when he'd realized that his mother wasn't going to be there to celebrate him becoming a teenager. We'd never spoken about it, but I'd seen his hurt. Rhett had carried the pain of his mother leaving all of his life and he'd never been able to speak about it. Not really. Yes, we'd talked about it on a superficial level, but he'd never opened up about her completely and I'd never pushed it.

"There's nothing you could do that would stop me from loving you, Rhett Madison." I squeezed his hand. "When is this class?"

"We can go tonight." He smiled sweetly. "They have it every day. It's a group setting."

"A group setting?" I knew my face reflected my horror. "What?"

"Haha, I know." He laughed. "That's what I thought as well, but supposedly it's meant to help to be around other couples with other issues and we all get to weigh in and discuss the issues."

"I see." I made a face. I wasn't sure how I felt about discussing our issues with other couples there. It seemed so impersonal.

"We'll see how it goes." His eyes searched mine. "We'll see if it helps."

"I'm willing to try." I nodded. "I'm surprised you even found the class, you surprise me."

"I'm a man of surprises."

"In your pants?" I joked and he laughed.

"Isn't that supposed to be my line?"

"WELCOME, WELCOME EVERYONE." A tall lady with short, curly black hair grinned at everyone in the room. "I'm Tasha and I'm the group lead today. Thanks to everyone for coming."

"Thanks for having us." Rhett answered and she beamed at him. I tried not to roll my eyes as I noticed some of the other girls in the class checking him out. No wonder their relationships were in trouble, if they were busy checking my man out.

"So is everyone ready to get started?" Tasha smiled.

"Yes," We all chorused and she sat down.

"Great." She looked at each of us and then continued. "Today is going to be hard for some of you. We aren't like most group meetings. We don't introduce ourselves and talk about our love of basketball or golf. We jump right into the issues. We try and get to the crux of the problems in your relationships. This setting is meant to help you identify your issues by listening to each other speak."

"People are going to tell me what me and Juan's problem is?" A girl to the right of Rhett spoke up. "How they going to know?"

"No, no, Valentina." Tasha smiled and looked at all of us. "But that was a great question. Let me explain how it's going to work.

We will go in turns and talk about our relationships. We will identify as a group, what issues we think each couple is facing and each couple will then spend some time and talk about whether or not they think they have that issue. Does that make sense everyone?"

"Yes," I nodded as Valentina made a face at me. I could see Rhett looking at me and I reached over and grabbed his hand. This was not exactly what I'd had in mind when I thought of a relationship course, but I was trying not to judge the class before it was over.

"Okay, let's start." Tasha nodded to me and Rhett. "Why don't you two start?"

"Yes, Brad and Angelina, I wanna know what problems you two have?" Valentina cracked a joke and the group laughed. Tasha held up her hand and looked around the group. "Remember this is a no judgment zone, I don't want any couples making fun of other couples issues, okay? You're all here because you're having problems in your relationship. Please don't say anything you wouldn't want to hear. Does everyone understand?"

"Si." Valentina said and rolled her eyes. I looked over at Rhett and he grinned at me. I could tell from his expression that he felt as out-of-place in this setting as I did. In fact, he looked so out of place that I wanted to laugh. Never in a million years, would I have pictured my Rhett in a group relationship class.

"Are you ready Rhett and Clementine?"

"Yes." I spoke up and Rhett squeezed my hand. "What exactly are we meant to say?"

"Just tell us about your relationship and we'll go from there."

"Okay," I nodded and took a deep breath. "Rhett and I have been best friends since we were little kids. I was the studious kid, always studying and never dating and he was the playboy, dating around and barely studying." I gave him a quick look. "And when I say he dated, he really dated. He would call me every night and tell me about his dates."

"Or I would go over to her place and tell her." He laughed. "And ask her for advice and help."

"Yeah, he recruited me to help him one night that he had two dates." I laughed remembering the past. "I know it sounds weird now, but that was the relationship we had. We could say anything to each other. We could do anything and we knew the other one wouldn't judge us." I paused and took a deep breath. "And then a few months ago, we realized we liked each other as more than friends."

"I realized I loved her as more than an annoying bratty sister." He added and I punched him in the arm. Tasha smiled at us and I continued.

"So we realized we loved each other and decided to give a relationship a chance. And we moved here from South Carolina and—"

"Do you two live together?" Valentina asked curiously.

"Yes, why?" I responded.

"You've been dating for a couple of months and you live together already?" She raised her eyebrows. "That's a bit fast, no?"

"We've been friends for years, so the relationship while new, isn't new new. We still knew each other."

"And how is living together going?" Tasha asked.

"It's fine." I said and at the same time that Rhett replied. "She's messy as hell."

"What?" I turned to him. "You're the messy one." I glared.

"I'm just saying you leave your clothes everywhere." He shrugged. "And your hair products and your makeup and your magazines."

"I don't leave them everywhere."

"It would be nice to have some order in the apartment?" He gave me a weak smile.

"I'm not messy." My voice rose in shock. "I don't even know where that is coming from."

"It's not a big deal, but I didn't realize that you were a slob."

I dropped his hand and moved away from him, feeling angry. How dare he call me a slob?

"So okay, the living arrangement seems to have some contention?" Tasha continued. "What about the rest of the relationship. How is that going?"

"What relationship? He just wants sex." I spat out.

"What?" Rhett's voice sounded shocked. "Are you joking?"

"Nope." I looked around the group. "I feel like all you care about is sex, that's the only time you act lovey dovey."

"I tell you I love you all the time." He sounded dazed. "Are you kidding me? I've never told a girl I love her before. You're the only one Clementine. You're my only real girlfriend."

"He doesn't treat me like a girlfriend. He doesn't plan dates. He doesn't buy me gifts. He doesn't surprise me with calls or poems or anything. All he does is ask what's for dinner and when he can have sex."

"Are you frigging kidding me?" He sounded angry. "I just brought you home some candy and dinner the other night."

"A Hershey's bar and a slice of pizza are not dinner and candy, Rhett." I sighed. "I mean I just felt like there would be more romance." I sighed and looked at Tasha. "I've never really been in a relationship before and I guess I had dreams of it being something a bit more."

"Welcome to the club, girlfriend." Valentina spoke up. "Juan and I have been together for five years and I'm still waiting for the romance. We had a baby the first year and I feel like that was it."

"Why is that?" Tasha spoke up, her eyes gleaming. I could tell she was happy that people were talking.

"I feel like Juan got the milk for free and now he doesn't want to buy the cow." Valentina made a face. "He won't marry me and I just feel like he just expects me to be there because I have little Juanita."

"I love you and Juanita." Juan spoke up. "I told you. I'm not going to marry you until I can afford a wedding."

"But you had a baby with her." I spoke up. "Why didn't you wait to have a baby until you were able to get married."

"It's not my fault she lied about being on the pill." He shrugged. "I take care of my baby." He looked at Tasha. "I'm a good dad."

"That's good." Tasha nodded. "And we'll get to you and Valentina soon, but let's keep this on Rhett and Clementine. I think we already have our first connection here, don't you guys?"

"Huh?" I looked at her in confusion. "We do?"

"You and Rhett have moved in with each other too early." Tasha nodded. "Rhett is not wooing you or taking you on dates because there is no need. He doesn't need to do any of that because he's already getting what he needs from you."

"I'm not just with her for sex." Rhett spoke up and I could tell from his voice that he was getting annoyed.

"You might not be with her for sex, but your end goal is sex and she's already giving it up." Valentina made a face. "There's no reason for you to put any effort in 'cos she's spreading her legs whenever you want some."

"Now now." Tasha shook her head. "Let's be careful with the language we're using and the statements we're making."

"It's not like I said he's getting head whenever he wants." Valentina looked annoyed and Tasha gasped. "Sorry." Valentina laughed and I could see Juan rubbing her thigh.

Tasha turned to me. "I can see a lot of love in your relationship and I think the issues you two face are clear. You've made the move from friends to lovers without fully understanding what that means. You can't just have the same relationship you had before. It's not going to work for either of you, but that isn't bad. It just means that you'll grow stronger in other ways."

"Yeah, I guess we'll have to figure it out."

"Okay. Now here's the tough part." Tasha stood up and handed us both a piece of paper. "I want you both to write down your number one concern in the relationship and then I want you to read it out loud." She handed us two pens. "Write, now." She instructed us and we both scribbled on the paper quickly. "Okay, done?" She asked and we both nodded. "I want you to read out what you've written down. You first, Clementine."

I cleared my throat and read quickly. "I'm scared that Rhett is going to miss the life of being a player and is going to want to be with another girl. I'm scared he's either going to cheat on me or he's going to lose interest." I said softly and Tasha nodded.

"You now Rhett." There was silence for a few seconds and then Rhett spoke up.

"I'm scared that Clementine is going to realize that I'm not good enough for her. I'm scared she's going to grow tired of me. I'm scared she's going to find someone better. I'm scared that I'm not good enough and she's going to leave me." He stopped and I felt my heart beating rapidly at his words. I turned to look at him and we both stared at each other, fear and love in our eyes. It was hard voicing our fears, but it was also hard listening to the other person as well. As we sat there, we both knew that both of our fears were valid in different ways. We loved each other, but our relationship was more complex than that. We were more complex than our base feelings. We'd been in each other's lives for so long, yet we'd never had an intimate relationship like this. Neither one of us had been prepared for the other issues to creep up into the relationship so quickly. But then again, neither one of us had any real experience with relationships.

"I'm so glad you were both honest with your issues." Tasha beamed at us and there was an understanding in her eyes. "That's the most important first step. Being honest means that there is hope. There is hope for both of you. We just need to get to the root of those problems."

We sat back and smiled and nodded, but I knew she was simplifying how far we'd come. Yes, we had acknowledged we had issues. However, getting to the root of the problems was going to be a much harder feat than just acknowledging them.

Seven

RHETT

Homesick is hard when you don't know
Just where it is that you call home.
I don't know how this roof's going to hold.
It's oh so cold.
It's been snowing too hard I fear.
Yes, I know that it's pretty here,
And the air is clear.
But the years aren't passing fast enough this way.
Maybe you can save me now.
I'm not sure how.
I'm calling out for that
I'm crying out for that.

"HOMESICK" BY DAVID BERKELEY—*SOME KIND OF CURE*

I sat with the phone cradled next to my ear feeling nothing. Absolutely nothing. And it scared me more than I wanted to admit to myself. I stared at the wall in front of me wishing that Clementine was home, but she was at school still.

"Can you come home?" The voice was impersonal. "She's not in a good way."

"What can I do if I come back to South Carolina?" My voice sounded cold, but I didn't know how to sound any other way.

"Maybe you can talk to her. She has Cirrhosis of the liver." He sounded bored as if he were talking about an everyday cough. "If she doesn't stop drinking, she's going to die."

"How long has she known?" I had to know the answer.

"Two years." He said without a change in his tone. I wondered how many times the doctor had made this call to family members. How many times he had had to tell someone that a loved one was dying and it was all their own fault.

"I see." I blinked and all I could think about was Clementine. Where was she? Was she with Holden? How ironic that she was worried about me cheating on her when she was the one that was hanging out with other guys. I knew I was being irrational. I knew that she was just studying with him, but I also knew now for a fact that he wanted her.

"Rhett, I know this is hard for you. I know you just moved, but it could really help if you came down. I'll let you think about it and see what you can do. Feel free to call the office if you have any questions, Rhett. You're her only family." And then just like that, he hung up.

My face was cold, my stomach felt heavy, the tears sat in the bottom of my eyes, wanting to fall. I could feel the vein in my upper thigh throbbing as I sat there. I felt nothing inside. Nothing, but a big empty void of pain. I felt like I'd just cut my arm off. I felt like I'd lost a part of myself. And I had no one to talk to. No one would be able to understand how I felt. I didn't want to hear that things would get better. I didn't want to hear that she loved me underneath it all. I didn't want to hear that I was better off without her. The truth of the matter was that she was my mother and all I wanted, was for her to love me. All I wanted was for her to say I was enough. I was enough reason to stop drinking. I was enough for her to get her act together. I wanted to be her little boy. I wanted to be the apple of her eye. I wanted to be enough to take the pain away. Didn't she realize how much I loved her? Didn't she know how much I wanted to take away her pain? Didn't she know that she was killing herself as well as me? Didn't she know that I'd give it all up, everything to just understand why?

She was killing herself with the alcohol, but I was the one dying inside. Nothing mattered without her love. Nothing could make up for the emptiness inside. Not even Clementine. No matter how many kisses she gave me. No matter how tightly she held me. No matter how many times she told me she loved me. She couldn't fix this. She couldn't make this better. I didn't even know what to do. What could I do if I went home? How could I make things better? I didn't even know where I belonged any more. Clementine was flourishing in Boston. She was blooming before my eyes and a part of me wondered if she even needed me anymore. And my mother? I didn't even know if she was really my mother anymore. Yes, she'd given birth to me, but she hadn't been in my life. I could barely remember what she looked like. I had to close my eyes and think hard to try and remember her face. My heart ached as I realized I didn't know where I belonged or how I belonged. I wanted somebody to save me. I wanted somebody to show me the way. I wanted Clementine to make it alright, but I didn't know if she could save me. I didn't even know if it was right for me to expect her to save me. I was the man. I was the one that was supposed to have it all together. I was scared for her to see the pain inside. I was scared of how she was going to react. How could I tell her how empty I felt inside? How could I tell her that behind my bravado and charisma, there was a shell of a man? How could I tell her that I loved her more than life itself, but something in me was still hurting? Something in me was constantly worried. I didn't even understand it myself. No one knew what lay behind my blue eyes. No one knew that every morning there was a dull ache that never went away. I didn't know how to tell her that I was scared that she was going to leave me because my mother had left me. If my own mother hadn't thought I was enough, how could I expect Clementine to feel any differently?

I stared at the phone in my hand and realized that, like it or not, my life was changed forever. Everyone thought that falling in love with Clementine had been the event that had changed my life. They thought the fact that I'd finally taken a girlfriend meant my life had taken a huge turn. And it had taken a turn. I was now in a relationship. But the relationship didn't define me. The relationship hadn't changed my life because Clementine had always been there in my heart. She'd always been mine and I'd been hers. There was never a real question about that. But now, now everything was different. I felt different. I felt lost. I felt like an evolution was going on in my life and I didn't want it anymore. I didn't want to know this new life. I didn't want my life to change. I didn't want to acknowledge that my mother was dying and even more than that, I didn't want to acknowledge that I needed to let that relationship go before it destroyed me.

Clementine and her family had always been my home. They'd been the one's there to pick me up and save me every time I fell, but that hadn't stopped the hole within from growing bigger and bigger. I didn't know what to do anymore. I was scared and worried. I was scared that I'd never be able to make it right. I didn't want to see my mother. I didn't want to face that pain again. I wanted to ignore it and her and that made me feel guilty. What sort of son was I? Was I capable of love? Was I capable of really loving someone? I didn't even know anymore. I just didn't even know. I jumped up and walked to the bedroom and looked at some of the photos that Clementine had put on the wall of the two of us. Photos that reminded me of the past. Photos that reminded me of how simple my life had been before I'd acknowledged that I had feelings for Clementine. The days when all I'd needed was to hook up with some random girl, to forget the loneliness. The days when casual sex had provided me with a high that was enough to get me through. Though, it had never been the sex that had gotten me through. It had always been Clementine. It had always been there. She'd always been my rock, but what had I been to her? Was I doomed to ruin this relationship? Could I be the man that she wanted? I stared at a photo of the two of us sitting on a couch together making silly faces and my heart broke. This beautiful girl was my life. She deserved better than me. She deserved a man that could give her the stars and the moon. She deserved a man that could give her everything she wanted. I didn't know if I was capable of being that man. I didn't know if I had it in me to give that much of my heart and soul; no matter how much I wanted to. I didn't even know if I had that much to give anymore. I sat down on the bed and held the picture frame to my chest. I wanted so much to make it work with Clementine, but I didn't know if I could ever be the man that deserved to be with her.

Eight

RHETT

"Did it hurt you? These are the scars you never show. She is a fire sign, you know. One day you're near and then you go."

"FIRE SIGN" BY DAVID BERKELEY—AFTER THE WRECKING SHIPS.

There was only one room with a light shining through the door as I walked down the corridor and I paused outside the door, debating whether or not I should go inside. My heart was racing as I stood there uncertainly. I wasn't even sure what I was doing here. I knew Clementine would wonder where I was when she got home. I hadn't called and I hadn't left a message, but I hadn't known what to say.

"Hey," a girl standing by the doorway nodded at me unsmiling. "You here for the group?"

"Perhaps."

"What's your issue?" She looked me up and down. "Let me guess, cocaine?"

"No, I don't do cocaine." I shook my head.

"Heroine?"

"No."

"Meth?" Her voice rose and she looked surprised. "You look too preppy for a meth addict."

"I'm not an addict."

"Then why are you here?" She sounded annoyed.

"To understand." I said softly.

"To understand what?"

"What it's like to be an addict."

"Oh." She pulled her hair to her lips and started sucking on it.

"Why are you here?" I smiled. "Addicted to sucking your hair?" I teased her lightly.

"Alcohol." She shrugged and looked down. "And company."

"Company?" I looked around the room. Most people were sitting in chairs by themselves, not communicating.

"It's not Glee Club." She said shrilly. "But we all come every week. I can count on them."

"For what?"

"To be there." She shrugged.

"I see." Though I didn't really. I looked at the small group of people and looked back at the door. "I guess I should leave." I said softly, the most unsure I'd ever been in my life.

"You don't have to leave." She shook her head, her eyes disappointed. "We could always use another member."

"I'm not an addict though. I don't want to take time away from anyone else."

"But you came to understand right?" She asked softly as I nodded. "I wish my boyfriend would come."

"You have a boyfriend?" I looked at her skinny body and greasy hair and had to admit I was surprised. "Sorry that was rude." I said quickly.

"No need to apologize." She laughed. "It takes a lot more than that to get me down."

"I didn't mean to be rude. Clementine says I talk without thinking sometimes."

"Who's Clementine? Your girl?" She looked at me thoughtfully.

I nodded in response, feeling guilty that I was even here. For some reason I felt like I was cheating on Clementine. I knew she'd be hurt if she knew I was here, but I hadn't known how to tell her how I felt. I was ashamed of myself for my feelings. I was ashamed that a part of me just wanted to forget my mother even existed. I was ashamed that I felt so empty inside, when I should have been the happiest in my life.

"She pretty?" The girl in front of me continued sucking her hair. "She must be real pretty if she got a guy like you."

"A guy like me?"

"A guy with big blue eyes and a handsome face." She laughed. "I'm an addict. I'm not blind."

"I'm really not all that." I said modestly and then laughed. I could imagine the face Clementine would have made if she'd witnessed this conversation.

"So is Clementine the one with the problem?" The girl paused. "Let me guess, she's addicted to crack and you don't know how to tell your blue-blood parents that their perfect son is caught up with a crackhead from the wrong side of the tracks."

"I'm no blueblood." I said with a drawl and laughed at her shocked expression. "And Clementine is not a crackhead or from the wrong side of the tracks."

"So who's the dope head?"

"No one's a dope head." I said softly.

"Oh." I knew she wanted to ask more, but she thought better of it.

"My mom's an alcoholic." I said softly. "And she's dying."

"Oh." She said again and this time she removed the hair from her mouth and brushed it away from her face. I could see now that she was prettier than I'd initially thought. "That's tough."

"I don't understand why she won't stop drinking." I said softly. "That's why I'm here. I want to understand. I want to feel compassion." My heart broke as I spoke. "I want to feel whole."

"Abuse? Rape? Repressed mental trauma? Depression?" She said softly. "Those things usually lead to alcoholism. At least they did to mine."

"I'm sorry." I said awkwardly, having forgotten that she also had an alcohol problem.

"Don't worry about it. My boyfriend Jim says stuff to me all the time." She shrugged. "Way more hurtful, but I still love him."

"What's your name?"

"Caroline."

"I'm Rhett."

"Like Rhett Butler in *Gone With The Wind*?"

"Just like Rhett Butler." I nodded.

"I should have guessed from your drawl." She looked at her watch. "We should grab a seat, Bill will be here soon and he likes to start right away."

"Maybe I should go." I said again, uncertainly. I wasn't even sure why I'd ended up here. I wasn't sure what I was expecting to figure out.

"Don't go." She grabbed my arm, her eyes pleading with me. "Maybe you'll find some answers."

"I doubt it."

"You never know. It helps me to come." She gave me a wistful smile, her eyes looking suddenly bleak. "These meetings are like a glimpse of sunshine in my grey days."

"Oh, I don't—"

"I sound depressing, don't I?" She giggled suddenly. "Jim always tells me to smile. He says that's my best asset."

"Then you should never stop smiling."

"We're high school sweethearts you know. You wouldn't think it by looking at me now, but I was head cheerleader and he was a part of the football team."

"All-American couple."

"We were Homecoming King and Queen." She stared off in the distance. "Of course I knew we would be."

"That's great."

"I bet you and Clementine were King and Queen as well right?" She looked at me then. "There's no way you weren't."

"We didn't date in high school." I said softly, thinking back to my friendship with Clemmie in high school. I couldn't believe how blind I'd been. "I was a bit of a doofus and didn't realize until recently that I loved her."

"Wow."

"We've been best friends for years." I continued. "And a part of me has always loved her, but I just didn't realize just what she meant to me."

"Why isn't she here?" She looked at me questioningly. "I'm surprised she didn't come as well."

"She doesn't know I'm here." I took a deep breath. "She doesn't know that my mom is dying."

"I'm sorry." Caroline grabbed my hand. "I didn't mean to be insensitive."

"It's fine." I shrugged. "I came because I want to understand why I feel the way I do. My heart is breaking and at the same time I feel a cold indifference." The words came out of my mouth reluctantly. It felt like I was letting out a secret I was ashamed of. A secret I didn't want anyone to know about. "And I think that my feelings towards my mother are hurting my relationship with Clementine."

"What does she say?"

"She doesn't know." I said softly. "I don't know how to tell her that I feel empty inside. I don't want to hurt her. I don't know how to explain that even though I love her with all my heart, there are days that my heart feels empty and void." I whispered the words feeling ashamed.

"Love's weird." She nodded. "I love Jim, but you know, the alcohol is something I love as well."

"I just want to be able to heal my heart." I sighed. "I just want to get over the hurt my mom left me with and I guess I came here because I think understanding her problem will help me to forgive her. And forgiving her will help me get rid of this void she left me with. And once I get rid of that void, I can get over the fear that Clementine might leave me."

"I understand." Caroline nodded, her eyes full of tears. "I'm scared that Jim might leave me too. He's the only one I have now. I just need to be a better person. I just need to give up the drink. If I could just go back to a time when I didn't drink, I'd be okay. We'd be okay. Jim and I could be okay. I just need to turn back time. I just need to go back to a day I didn't drink, then I could make sure I never picked up a bottle."

"I'm sure Jim understands how hard you're trying." I squeezed her arm and she looked at me then, her eyes clouded over.

"I just wish I could do my life over." She whispered and we walked over to the chairs.

"BYE CAROLINE." I waved as she ran out of the room as soon as the session had ended. I was sad that she'd just left like that, but I guessed that her boyfriend was most probably waiting on her to come home. Just like Clementine. I felt guilty that I'd left the apartment without letting her know I'd be gone, but I was so thankful that I'd come here. I didn't fully understand what it was to be an addict, but I'd seen the pain that many of the group were dealing with and I was beginning to understand how complex the issue of addition was. I turned to Bill the instructor and spoke, "Thanks for having me here. I really appreciate you letting me sit in."

"We were glad to have you Rhett. You should really check out some Nar-Anon groups." He handed me some papers. "I think you'll find that it's helpful being around other people that have family members that are addicts. "It's important for you to not take on the addiction issue and let it control your life."

"I think I'm going to look for a group." I nodded, thankfully. "I was glad to come today though. I know this might sound weird, but I feel calmer after having been here. I really liked everyone, especially Caroline."

"And Caroline really took to you. It's been a while since I've seen her smiling like that." Bill said.

"Oh, she seems really nice." I nodded. "I hope her boyfriend comes to a meeting soon to support her."

"Her boyfriend?" He looked confused.

"Jim." I said, hoping I wasn't sharing private information. "Caroline was talking about him earlier."

"Oh." He nodded and sighed. "I see."

"What?" I leaned forward. "Is he some sort of asshole?"

"No." He paused and then looked me in the eyes. "Jim is dead, Rhett. He died in a drunk driving accident, Caroline was the one driving."

"Oh." The blood drained from my face. "I didn't know."

"He's been dead for four years." He nodded. "They were teenagers. She has a hard time coping."

"She doesn't still drink does she?"

"No." He shook his head. "She never had another drop after Jim died."

"I didn't know." I said again, feeling my heart sinking. "I wish she'd said something, I..." My voice trailed off.

"It's better that you didn't know." He reached out and rubbed my shoulder. "She was able to be herself for the afternoon. She was able to forget. She was able to be a normal girl for a few hours."

"She's not normally like that?"

"She rarely speaks. It's still hard for her." He sighed. "We all become addicts for different reasons and we all cope with our addictions and actions differently. We all try the best we can. Unfortunately, sometimes it's not enough."

"At least you all have each other."

"Yeah, many times, those that aren't addicts don't understand." He smiled at me. "That's why it's so great that you're trying to figure out what your mom's going through."

"Yeah." I looked at the clock. "I should go." I stepped back. "Sorry, I have to go." I hurried to the door and ran down the hallway, needing to exit the building as soon as I could. I paused as I reached the door and I stood there for a second feeling sad as I thought about Caroline. I couldn't even imagine the pain she must live with every day. I'd die if anything ever happened to Clementine. And if I'd been the person to cause something bad happening to her? Well, I didn't know if I could live with myself. I felt sad as I thought about Caroline, but then realized just how strong she was. She was living with demons, but she'd stopped drinking. That had to be hard. I could only imagine how hard it was. And then I thought about my mom. She didn't have anyone. And I had been ready to give up on her. I understood now that giving up on her was giving up on us. I knew that I needed to see her again. I needed to get my answers from her. I had to go back home, but before I could do that, I needed to speak to Clementine. I needed her to know what was going on. I needed her to know that although I was the happiest I'd ever been in my life, I was also the saddest. I needed her to know that even though there was an us, there no longer felt like there was a me. I was lost and while I knew my way to her heart, I didn't know my own way back home again. I knew who I was when I was with her, but when I was by myself, I had no idea who I really was. I needed to go back home. I needed to make things right with my mom. And I needed to find myself. As I realized what I needed to do, I felt my heart breaking. I had no idea how Clementine was going to take everything.

"CLEMENTINE, I WROTE a poem for you. Yes, I, Rhett Madison love you Clementine O'Hara more than I've ever loved anyone before. And I wrote a poem for you." My voice caught as I stared into her sad eyes.

"I don't believe it." She smiled weakly. I could tell she was still upset that I'd come home so late. But she seemed to understand that after the call from the doctor about my mom that I'd needed to get out and get some fresh air.

"Believe it." I smiled at her beautiful face. "Clementine," I took a deep breath. "I have to go back to South Carolina."

"For how long?" She looked like she was fighting tears and I could feel a sharp pain in my chest. It almost felt like we were breaking up.

"I don't know." I took her hands into mine. "I need to work this stuff out with my mom, once and for all. I need to try and find a way to battle the pain I feel."

"She loves you, you know that right?"

"Honestly, no, no I don't know." I said sadly. "All my life, I've pushed my pain and rejection to the side. I've pretended it didn't matter, but it does matter. It matters a lot and it hurts. I feel like a part of me doesn't even exist. I feel like a part of me has always been lost. And the only reason all of me isn't lost is because of you. You're my map home. You're my compass. You're my everything. Without you, there would be absolutely nothing in my life worth living for. And that's powerful, Clementine. That's not healthy. I live to be with you. I live for you. I'm empty without you. And I can't be empty without you. I can't be empty because you need a man that is full. You need a man that can give you all those things you've always dreamed about. I was a boy, Clementine. But now, now I need to be a man."

"I don't want you to go." She bit her lower lip and I could see the tears in her eyes. "I don't want her to hurt you. She loves you, but I don't know if she'll ever be the person you need her to be, Rhett."

"That's okay. That's why I'm going. I need it to be okay. I need to be able to accept that." I sighed. "I need to do this for myself. I need to do this to try and get some closure. I need to make myself whole. I need to be the man you need me to be."

"I only want you Rhett. I'll take you however you are." She said quietly and I could see the tears flowing from her eyes. "I don't want to be without you."

"I have something to ask you, Clementine."

"What?" Her eyes searched mine and I took a deep breath.

"You've always been my best friend. You're the love of my life. I know things are different between us now and I know I'm not the most romantic of men. I want to make a promise to you, Clemmie. I want you to know that I'm yours forever, as long as you'll have me. I love you more than anything. I wrote this poem for you and I want to read it to you, but first I had a question."

"Yes." She said quietly.

"Clementine, I know it's too soon to ask you to marry me, but I want to make a promise to you. I want to promise you that I'll always be by your side. I want to be your husband Clemmie and I'd like you to promise me that one day you'll consider being my wife."

"I'd very much love to be your wife one day, Rhett." She smiled and gave me a quick kiss. "Even though this isn't a proposal, I'm still deeply touched." She gave me a wide smile as her eyes teased me and I chuckled. "And yes, yes, I'll be your wife." And then she started laughing. "Am I being too enthusiastic for a non-proposal?"

"You can never be too enthusiastic." I grinned, then gave her a quick kiss. "Now shh, let me tell you my poem before I get stage fright." I took a deep breath and then said the poem I remembered by heart. Her eyes gazed at me adoringly as I said the words from my heart and I knew in that moment that I was already a different man than I'd been just six months before. I was only at the beginning of my journey, but I knew in my gut that I was on the right path.

"There's not a day that goes by,
That I don't remember your eyes,
The first time you said you loved me
And the last time we said goodbye.

I love you more than the stars in the sky
I love you so much, I believe I can fly
You are the dot to my i

I am the apple in your pie.

I'm not a poet, like Frost or Cummings
I'm not a writer like Hemmingway or Poe
I can't build you a house with my bare hands
But I love you so much more than you know.

Each hair on your head is precious
Each breath that you take keeps me sane
Each part of me loves every part of you and I'll say it over and
over again.

I love you, Clementine O'Hara.
You stole my heart and I never want it back
You are my reason for living.
You are the joy in my heart.

I promise you that I'll always love you.
I promise you that you'll always be mine.
I promise that with each step that we take.
I'll always be by your side.

We have an eternity to love each other.
We have a love that is pure
You are my soul mate, my better half and
Nobody could love you more."

"I love you, Clemmie. Thank you for agreeing to be my wife.
Thank you for everything." I pulled her into my arms and I could
feel her tears on my cheek as she cried. "Happy tears, right?"

"Of course, happy happy tears." She grabbed ahold of my face
and kissed me hard. "Always happy tears with you, Rhett."

"And I'm not going to be gone for long." I promised as I kissed her. "This is just the start of a new journey in our life. This is just the start of our epic love story, you know that right?"

"No Rhett." She kissed my lips. "This isn't the start. This is just the end of part one and the beginning of part two."

"I like that." I kissed her back. "I like that a lot. This is the beginning of part two. And I promise you Clementine, that part two is going to blow your mind. Part two is going to be the most epic of love stories. Part two is going to make you love me more than you already do."

"I don't know if that's possible, Rhett. I already love you more than life itself." She stroked my face and played with my hair. "But I'm here for the ride, let's see what you got."

PART II

Nine

RHETT

The silence of your thoughts can be overwhelming. Leaving Clementine and taking a plane back to South Carolina was the hardest thing I've ever had to do. It felt like I was leaving her forever and all I could think about was the look in her eyes as she tried not to cry. She was trying to be strong for me and I loved her even more for that. Driving the rental car back to my house felt weird. I didn't even know what I was doing. All I could think about was Clementine: What was she doing? What was she thinking? Did she miss me? Would she be happier without me? My thoughts were sad, but it was better than the alternative. It was better than thinking about my mother. I wasn't looking forward to our reunion. I wasn't looking forward to having to deal with my feelings. Not at all.

I pulled up to my house and walked inside, feeling like a different person to the one I'd been when I left. I turned on the lights and walked to the kitchen to find something to eat. My heart exploded when I saw trays of food with a note on top.

"Clementine told me you were coming home. Here's some food to last you for a couple of days. Then I expect you to come and see me. I've missed you and want to see you soon.

Lots of love,
Nanna

P.S. Clemmie told me to make you an apple pie as well, so enjoy it. I've been slaving away for hours."

I closed the fridge and pulled my phone out.

"Hello." Clementine's voice was soft and I wished that I was there with her.

"Hello, I made it ho... back." I walked to the living room, not sure why I hadn't been able to say home. Though, I guessed this was no longer my home.

"How are you?"

"Good, Nanna left me food."

"Good, have you eaten yet?"

"I just got in, Clemmie." I laughed.

"You need to eat."

"I miss you." I sat back on the couch and closed my eyes and pictured her face. "I wish you were here."

"I wish I was there as well."

"What are you doing?"

"I'm watching TV."

"Devious Maids?"

"It's not on." She laughed. "We watched the season finale, remember?"

"Not really." I laughed. "Is that when they were shouting and stuff?" I said trying to remember the episode I'd watched with her.

"They are always shouting and stuff." She laughed again.

"Oh those catty maids."

"You know you loved the show."

"I loved lying in bed with you and watching it, more like." I said honestly. "Give me football any day."

"What are you going to do tonight?"

"Sleep." I sighed and stood up. "Though that might be hard."

"Why?" She paused. "Sorry, I guess you're still upset over your mom."

"That's not why it's going to be hard to sleep." I laughed. "I was thinking about something else actually."

"Oh, what's that?"

"I was thinking that it's going to be hard to sleep without sleeping next to you."

"Oh, how sweet Rhett."

"I'd love to be inside of you right now." I continued and grunted. "I'd love to be making sweet love to you and watching you as you orgasm on top of me."

"Rhett." She admonished me with a slight smile. "That's not so sweet."

"Why not?" I laughed. "You should be happy that your boyfriend is telling you he wishes he was inside of you right now."

"Uhm, I should be happy about that why?" She said lightly.

"Because you know I'm thinking about you and not some other girl."

"Are you joking Rhett?" Her voice rose. "I should be happy because you're not mentally cheating on me?"

"I'm just saying. Lots of guys' fantasies revolve around other girls. Like playboy models and stuff."

"Rhett Madison, just when I think you're finally maturing you go and say something that reminds me that you're still a horn dog."

"A horn dog that wants to be fucking you right now."

"We went from sweet lovemaking to fucking in ten seconds." She giggled. "What am I going to do with you, Rhett?"

"Have phone sex with me." I jumped up on my bed and lay back. "And make it sexy as hell."

"Isn't phone sex sexy as it is?" She said lightly. "How do you make phone sex sexier than it already is?"

"Are you saying that you're willing to try?" I asked excitedly. "Because I can tell you how to make it hot as hell."

"Rhett." She paused. "I can't believe you're going to make me do this."

"Where are you?" I grinned into the phone. "And what are you wearing?"

"I already told you I'm watching TV. I'm sitting on the couch in the living room and I'm wearing a pair of jeans that I got at Old Navy before we left. Oh, skinny jeans by the way. I'm also wearing a Harvard sweatshirt, the one you bought me the first day we came to campus. Do you remember that day? It was when you said—"

"Clementine." I groaned. "A simple, I'm naked or a bra and panties would have sufficed."

"But I'm wearing more than that."

"Clementine, turn the TV off, walk to the bedroom. Take off your skinny jeans and take off your sweater, then tell me what you're wearing."

"I wanted to watch the end of this episode though." She sounded sad. "I think we're going to find out the winner."

"Winner of what?" I rolled my eyes in the dark as I slid my jeans off.

"Rachael vs. Guy: Kids Cook-off, tonight is the finale and I want to find out who wins."

"Is that a joke, Clemmie?" I growled into the phone. "Take your clothes off now."

"What?" She squeaked out in surprise.

"Turn the TV off and take your clothes off." I commanded her, enjoying my role. "And do it now."

"Are you joking?" She asked softly.

"No. I'm not joking." I said with authority and then I paused. "You asked how this could be sexier right?"

"Huh?" She sounded confused and I laughed.

"We're going to role-play tonight."

"Role-play?"

"Yes, tonight I'm your Dom over the phone. You will do exactly what I say and when."

"Uh?" She paused. "Rhett?"

"Is the TV still on?"

"Yeah, I just told you that I'm —"

"Turn the TV off now." I growled. "And get your ass to the bedroom and take your clothes off stat."

"How do you know what a Dom does?" She asked softly, but I knew she had turned the TV off because I no longer heard the noise in the background.

"I don't know, Clemmie." I groaned. "I mean I've seen a few pornos, but if you're asking if I've been a Dom before, the answer is no. I'm just guessing and it seems like it would be fun, a different sort of phone sex right?" I waited for her to answer, but there was silence on the other side of the phone. I sat up uncomfortably and wondered if I had pissed Clemmie off or scared her. "You there, Clemmie?" Silence met me again. "Clemmie, answer me. Are you mad at me?"

"I was just waiting for permission to speak, Sir." Clementine's voice held a hint of humor in it and I started laughing, suddenly feeling lighter than I'd felt in a long time.

"You may talk, Clemmie." I growled again, getting back into it. "Now go into the bedroom and take off your clothes and tell me exactly what you're doing."

"Yes, Sir." She whispered into the phone and I could hear her walking. I could hear her breathing increase as she started to take her clothes off and I closed my eyes again to try and picture her disrobing.

"Tell me what you're doing." I commanded as silence filled the phone again.

"I'm taking off my blue skinny jeans." She said awkwardly and I could just picture her face blushing as she talked.

"Are they off yet?"

"Yeah, I just pulled them off." She paused. "Now, I'm taking off my crimson Harvard sweater and throwing it onto the floor. Then I'm going to pick it up and hang it in the closet because my boyfriend says I'm messy."

'Too much information, Clemmie." I groaned as I smiled at her words. "What do you have on now?"

"I have on my bra and panties." She said seductively and I could feel myself growing hard at her lowered voice.

"What color panties?"

"I'm wearing the white panties with hearts that I got at Target. I think they are Hanes, but could be Fruit of the Loom. I forget."

"Don't you mean you're wearing a silky black thong?" I shook my head at her words.

"No...I mean yes." She said in a seductive voice again. "I'm wearing a silky black thong and a see through black bra that you can see my nipples through."

"Oh, I wish I could see you in it." My hand found its way into my boxers.

"I wish you could take them off of me." She continued. "I'm peeling my thong off now because it's wet because I'm thinking of you."

"Stop." I growled. "You can't take the thong off until I tell you."

"Oh, okay."

"Get onto the bed." I grabbed my cock and started rubbing slowly.

"I'm getting onto the bed now, Sir." She breathed into the phone as she made her way onto the mattress I'd shared with her just the night before. I rubbed myself harder as I pictured her on the bed with her legs spread, and lower lip trembling, waiting for me.

"I think we need to keep this Sir thing." I muttered into the phone. "It's hot as hell."

"I don't think so, Rhett." She giggled. "There is no way that I'm going to be calling you Sir for the rest of my life."

"Why not?" I laughed. "Don't you want to be my naughty schoolgirl?"

"Nope." She giggled.

"Shh." I grumbled. "Put your hand down the front of your thong and touch yourself. Tell me exactly what you feel when you touch yourself."

"Okay." She paused. "Uhm, can I take my panties off please, Sir? My granny panties aren't as easy to slip into as a thong would be."

"Clemmie," I groaned. "You need to get rid of all granny panties, ASAP, you hear me?"

"I'm not wearing a thong every day, Rhett. They are not comfortable. That piece of string up my ass all day is not something I want to get used to."

"Then don't wear panties."

"Yeah, that's going to happen." I knew she was rolling her eyes.

"Clemmie, just take your panties off."

"What about my bra?"

"Did I say you could take your bra off?"

"You're really getting off on bossing me around aren't you?"

"Did I give you permission to speak?" I asked softly.

"Enjoy yourself, Rhett." She muttered. "This is the last time I'm going to be your sub."

"You wouldn't make a very good sub." I laughed. "You don't like to listen."

"You wouldn't make a good Dom." She said. "It's not all about being a bossy boots."

"That's exactly what it's about." I grunted and she mumbled something under her breath that I didn't hear. "What did you say, Clemmie?"

"I said, I don't think a Dom would agree with you about that."

"Who cares?" I shrugged. "We both know I'm not really a Dom and we both know that you wouldn't make a good sub."

"Why wouldn't I make a good sub?"

"The fact that we are having this discussion after I told you to take off your bra and panties tells me all I need to know."

"You didn't tell me to take my bra off. You told me to take my panties off. I asked you if I can take my bra off as well, as I feel weird lying here on the bed in just my bra."

"Clementine. Take your bra off." I groaned. "And shut up."

"What?" Her voice rose.

"What are you wearing?" I asked softly. There was silence for a few seconds, but then she responded.

"I'm naked." She whispered. "And waiting for your commands, My Lord."

It took everything in me to not burst out laughing. *My Lord, my ass.* I could just picture Clementine's face as she lay there. And it made me fall in love with her even more. This was my Clementine; even though she was doing this for me, she just couldn't stop herself from making snide comments.

"Take your right hand and run it up to your left breast. Close your eyes and rub your palm across your nipple. Then take your two fingers and pinch it lightly. Imagine it's me touching you."

"Oh." She moaned and I knew she was doing as I asked.

"Now take your hand and do the same thing to your right breast. Tell me how you feel."

"I feel horny." She moaned and I groaned in response as I imagined my lips sucking on her nipples.

"Run your left hand down to your pussy as you continue playing with your right nipple." I groaned and shifted in the bed as I started getting harder. "Tell me what you feel."

"I feel moisture." She whispered.

"Where?"

"Down there." She moaned.

"Tell me." I groaned, my hand moving faster.

"In my private area."

"Tell me." I grunted louder.

"I feel wet in my pussy." She groaned and her breathing increased. "Oh Rhett."

"Are you touching yourself?" I asked softly, imagining her hand in her pussy.

"Yes."

"What are you doing?"

"I'm touching myself. Oooh." She whimpered.

"Are you playing with your clit?"

"Yes." She whispered.

"I didn't say you can play with your clit."

"I don't care." She moaned. "I wish you were here."

"I wish I was there as well." My hand was moving faster and faster. "If I was there I would spread your legs open and my tongue would be lapping up your juices. If I was there, my tongue would be inside of you now and I'd feel your pussy trembling on my face. I'd feel your whole body shuddering as I brought you to a climax with my tongue."

"Oh Rhett." She groaned. "Don't stop."

"Are you close to orgasm?" I asked softly, feeling myself growing harder and hornier.

"Yes," She whimpered. "I can imagine your breath on my pussy as you lick me, I can feel you teasing me with your tongue."

"Put a finger inside your pussy." I muttered. "Imagine it's my cock. Slide it in and out hard. Imagine it's me fucking you."

"Oh." She cried out.

"Go faster." I knew I was close to coming as I pictured Clementine on the bed fingering herself. I couldn't remember the last time I'd felt so close to having this powerful of a release without actually having sex.

"I'm flipping you over now." She cried out. "I'm flipping you over and getting on top of you. I'm sitting down on your hard cock now Rhett. And I'm riding you hard and fast."

"Keep going." I groaned.

"You're grabbing my hips and I'm leaning forward and brushing my breasts in your face. You're sucking my nipples and I'm grinding myself into you and I'm moving faster and faster."

"Yes, keep moving." I shouted in the verge of explosion.

"I'm coming on you now." She cried out. "Oh Rhett, I'm coming."

"Me too." I grunted as I exploded into my hand. "Oh shit, Clemmie, you're so fucking sexy."

"I love you, Rhett." She moaned.

"I love you too, Clementine." I rolled over and stretched.

"So that was pretty hot." She yawned. "Even if you suck as a Dom."

"I don't suck as a Dom, you suck as a sub."

"At least we can suck together." She laughed.

"I wish you were here right now to suck—"

"Rhett." She giggled. "Dirty old man."

"Only for you." I jumped up. "I should hop in the shower and change the sheets. I just had a mini-explosion."

"I should shower as well." She agreed.

"I miss you." I sighed as I realized that I was going to be all alone again.

"I miss you too, but I'll see you soon."

"Clemmie, don't have too much fun without me." I said quickly. "I don't want you to forget me."

"How could I forget you, Rhett Madison?" She paused. "Or should I say Dom Madison?"

"I'll have you screaming out the next time I see you, Clementine O'Hara."

"Do you promise?" She giggled.

"I more than promise." I growled into the phone. "The next time I take you, I'm going to make sure that you know this Dom doesn't play."

"I look forward to it." She said sweetly. "Good night, Rhett."

"Night Clemmie." And then we hung up and I was stuck in the darkness once again. All by myself.

Ten

RHETT

You know when you wake up and you don't want to get out of bed that you're not looking forward to the day. That moment when your eyes open, and you just want to close them, and fall back to sleep again indicates the moment when something is not right in your life. I'm not a psychologist or a philosopher, but I know what it feels like to be lost and alone. I know what it's like to not want to face the day. Ever since Clementine had come into my life, I'd had thoughts and memories that I could no longer shove to the side. I wasn't able to occupy my mind and time with frivolous girls and inane chatter with Tomas and the boys.

Ring Ring.

I groaned as I reached for my phone. Who was preventing me from going back to sleep?

"Good morning, Rhett."

"Clementine?" I groaned. "It's early."

"It's 8am there. It's time to get up."

"I don't want to get up yet."

"Don't make me come and wake you up."

"I wish." I laughed and sat up staring at the door. Was she here? Was she going to surprise me?

"You know I'd be there if I didn't have midterms." She said softly and my heart dropped. So maybe she wasn't here after all.

"Yeah, I know." I tried not to sound sad. I was starting to feel like a pitiful little boy and it was annoying me.

"What are you going to do today?"

"Not sure yet." I yawned and lay back down.

"You're not going to visit your mom?"

"Maybe not today."

"Oh." She paused. "I thought you went down there to talk to your mom."

"That doesn't mean I need to go and see her as soon as I arrive." I was irritated.

"I know, but you're not doing much else right?"

"I'll go when I'm ready." I said. "Anything else?"

"Don't be mad at me, Rhett."

"I'm not mad. I don't care. I already told you I'm in bed and trying to sleep. Just because you have to get up early because you're a super nerd, doesn't mean I have to get up early. Some of us like to have a lie in you know."

"Remember when we took that pottery class." She asked softly.

"What? What pottery class." I jumped out of the bed, feel antsy. "What are you talking about?"

"Do you remember when we were kids and we took that pottery class."

"Kind of." I sighed. "Why?"

"Remember how mad you were at me because my jar was perfectly shaped and I learned how to use the kiln before you. Remember how you made fun of me."

"No."

"Well you did. You got upset at me because you were frustrated. And it made me sad. I even cried a little bit, but then the next class we were laughing and you made the most beautiful piece and I—"

"What's the point of your story Clementine?" I snapped, annoyed.

"I love you, Rhett. You can take it out on me. I'm not going anywhere. I'm not going to turn my back on you. I understand."

Her voice was soft. "I'm not a little girl anymore, I'm not going to cry if you call me names."

"What names did I call you?"

"Super nerd."

"You are a nerd." I laughed. "I thought you were proud of that name."

"Oh yeah, every girl is proud of being a super nerd, though I suppose that's better than Queen nerd."

"What about Princess nerd?"

"No thanks."

"Darn." I laughed into the phone, feeling less tense. "I know what you just did."

"What?" She said innocently.

"You completely changed subjects to get my mind off of my mom."

"Would I do that?"

"Yes and thank you." I took a deep breath. "You're right of course, I need to go and see my mom right away. I need to try and get this all sorted out as soon as I can."

"You know everything might not work out as you want, right?" She asked softly.

"You mean my mom might not take me into her arms and tell me that all she wants is to be my mother and she's going to change for me?"

"I'm sorry." Her voice cracked and I knew she was close to tears. It saddened me and warmed my heart to know how deeply she felt my pain. I wasn't sure what I'd done to have been so lucky as to have found someone like Clementine. Someone that had taken me so completely into her heart that my pain was her pain, my joy was her joy and my love was her love.

"Don't be sorry, it's not your fault." I gripped the phone, not wanting her to know just how anxious I felt inside. "I remember, you know."

"You remember what?"

"The summer we took that pottery class." I paused. "And the summer you convinced me to take those cotillion dance classes with you."

"Well, I wanted to learn how to dance. And your father was offering."

"It was fun." A flash of a memory from the past hopped into my head and I started laughing. "Remember how you always tried to lead and Ms. Maggie always had to tell you, Clementine let Rhett lead."

"And I'd always tell her that was sexist." She giggled. "I wanted to know why a woman couldn't lead. It was easier to lead."

"And she always frowned when she saw us coming to class."

"No she didn't." Clementine was laughing now. "She used to frown at me. She loved you, with your bright blond hair and sky blue eyes. She used to call you her sunshine on a cloudy day."

"True, she loved me, didn't she?"

"Ugh." Clementine groaned. "She was a cougar."

"Clemmie, I was 15 and she was 35. I don't think she was interested in me romantically." I laughed.

"They're all interested in you Rhett." Her voice sounded nonchalant, but I knew her well enough to know that the memory of my past still upset her.

"But the only one I'm interested in is you, my dear."

"I'm horrible, aren't I?" She sighed. "I don't know how this conversation came to you cheering me up."

"Clemmie." I groaned. "Please don't ever think that your feelings aren't valid, just because I'm going through something as well."

"Where has my best friend gone and what have you done with him?" She exclaimed. "The Rhett Madison I knew could go on for days about his issues."

"My issues were superficial." I sighed, remembering how many conversations had revolved around me being annoyed that a girl was getting too comfortable and expectant with me.

"Well, I wouldn't say that exactly." She said and then giggled as I walked into the kitchen and opened the fridge. "What are you doing? Are you still in bed?"

"No, I'm not in bed, thank you Mom." I surveyed the fridge and sighed. "I'm in the kitchen looking for breakfast, but I have no bacon and eggs."

"You could go to Nanna's and she'll make you some fried chicken and grits."

"For breakfast?"

"Since when have you turned down fried chicken for breakfast?"

"I know." I laughed. "I wish you were here."

"So do I." We were both silent for a few seconds before she spoke up. "So what are you going to do today then?"

"I guess I'll go and see Nanna for those grits." I laughed and then closed my eyes. "And maybe I'll visit my mom as well."

"That would be good." She said softly.

"Yeah, the sooner I work things out with her, the quicker I can be back with you."

"Feel free to take your time."

"Why?" I felt a stirring of jealousy in my stomach. "So you can be with Holden?"

"Rhett." She sighed.

"Are you going to see him again?"

"You know he's my partner."

"Whatever."

"You can't be mad at me for this, Rhett."

"He wants you. You know this. He told you. He wants in your pants and I'm not even there to kick his ass."

"I don't want him."

"Isn't that what all girls say?" I muttered, annoyed again. "And then he slips his fingers into—"

"Rhett." She shouted angrily. "You're really pissing me off right now."

"I don't like you hanging out with his pompous ass. You already know that he's going to try something again."

"And I will say no again if he does."

"If you didn't like him, you wouldn't see him again."

"You're not being fair." She sounded agitated. "This is really unfair Rhett."

"How would you like it if I went to go and see Penelope?" I muttered. "What if I invited her over for lunch? How would that make you feel?"

"Seriously, Rhett? How old are you?" She muttered. "That's not funny and it's not even the same situation."

"Well, yes it is." I grunted, feeling out-of-sorts again. I knew I was being childish. I knew I was in the wrong, but the stubborn part of me didn't want to give in.

"Rhett, do you think this isn't hard for me as well?" She whispered into the phone. "Do you think worries don't cross my mind? Do you think I don't wonder what's going to happen if you see some hot blonde and she gives you a big smile? Do you think I'm not concerned that you're going to miss your playboy ways and just forget me?"

"I could never forget you, Clementine."

"You could forget me for a night quite easily." She sighed. "I mean, let's be honest here, you've lived that lifestyle for so long. You're vulnerable and I'm not there..." Her voice trailed off.

"You think I'd cheat on you?" I sat on the floor and leaned back against the fridge, my heart thumping as I realized that Clementine didn't trust me.

"No." Her voice was adamant. "I don't think you would because I love you and trust you, but I can't lie and say that some days are harder than others. However, I don't say anything because inherently I have to believe that you wouldn't do that."

"I don't think you would cheat on me either." I said slowly. "I just don't even know what to think or feel anymore."

"I wish I could fix it for you, Rhett. I wish I could fill that hole in your heart. I wish I could be all that you need." Her voice caught and I knew she was crying. My heart stilled at the sound of her tears.

"I'm going to go and see my mom." I took a deep breath and stood up. "I'm scared, but I don't want...." I couldn't say anymore. I didn't even know how to voice the feelings I felt inside. I didn't know how to explain the hate and the love I had for my mother. I didn't know how to explain the pain and worry that came from thinking about her.

"I know." She whispered. "I know Rhett. I'll be here, if you need to talk."

"I'll call you later." I felt a new sense of urgency running through me as I hung up the phone. What was I doing? This was the beginning of our relationship. This was meant to be the best time of our lives and I was ruining it. I was destroying our relationship and I didn't know how to fix it unless I dealt with my issues with my mother. I didn't want to see her. I didn't want to talk to her. I didn't want to deal with it. The only thing that was prodding me along was Clementine and her smile. I couldn't lose Clemmie, not now. Not when she owned my heart.

"HOW ARE YOU?" The words were so formal, yet I didn't know what else to say as I sat in front of my mother in her living room.

"Good now that you're here." She smiled at me eagerly as she sat back, her fingers moving back and forth in a jittery fashion.

"Okay." I looked away from her and tried not to think about how skinny she looked. Her hair looked thinner and her skin looked yellow. She looked worse than I remembered from a few months before.

"How is Clementine?" She leaned forward eagerly. "Is she coming over as well?"

"I told you, she's in Boston." I shook my head. "She's in school there."

"Oh yeah." She nodded and picked up her glass of water. "I remember."

"So what have you been up to?" I looked around the room, not wanting to ask her if she was still drinking.

"You know." She nodded.

"That's not an answer." I said, feeling tense inside. "What have you been up to? Are you working?"

"I'm working on getting clean." She said weakly.

"So you've stopped drinking?"

"I stopped." She nodded and she looked into my eyes. "I stopped."

"You have?" I asked her softly, staring into her eyes. "How long have you been sober?"

"Would you like something to eat?" She stood up slowly. "I have your favorite."

"My favorite?" I asked, my heart light. Had she remembered my favorite food?

"Fried okra." She nodded eagerly and my stomach dropped in disappointment.

"I don't like okra."

"Not even fried?"

"You know I hate okra. I've always hated okra." I was annoyed.

"Oh." She stood there awkwardly. "I must have forgot."

"Yeah."

"You're looking very handsome." She stared at me for a few seconds. "Very much like your dad when he was young."

"Thanks, I guess."

"I hated him you know." She made a face. "I never really loved him. I loved another guy, Bill, Bill Richards was his name." She paused and looked me in the eyes. "Or was his name Bill Harris?"

"I don't know."

"Now he was a handsome man. Went to West Point you know. He's something big in the Air Force now."

"Okay."

"How I love him." She sighed. "I wish I had married him now. He wanted to marry me you know. He wanted me to have his kids, but I chose your dad. He had more money and well, I got pregnant." She gave me a look and then turned away. "And your grandparents didn't believe in abortions."

I was silent as I stared at her. My face and body felt cold as she continued pacing the room.

"I think about it sometimes." She looked out of the window. "What would my life have been like if I'd done things differently? Would I be happier? Would I have a life full of beautiful kids that loved me and took care of me?" Her voice was bitter. "Things would have been different."

As I sat there, with my fists clenched, all I could think about was the fact that I should have stayed in bed. Why had I come? I should have just stayed in bed.

"Do you want a drink?" She turned to me, her face blank.

"What?"

"A drink?"

"A drink of what?" I asked softly as she looked at me. The only thing was, her eyes didn't really see me. She was looking at me, but I could tell she wasn't actually seeing me. There was such a look of bitterness and hatred in her eyes that it scared me.

"Do you have any money?" She smiled weakly. "I can go and get you a drink."

"I don't need a drink."

"Do you have any money?" Her voice sounded more urgent.

"What do you need money for?"

"I just want a Goddamn drink, what the fuck? Just leave me alone." She screamed. "I just want a Goddamn drink, I don't need to answer to you."

"Mom," I took a deep breath. "I thought you didn't drink."

"Why can't I drink? Everyone can drink? I need to drink." She started crying. "Everyone always judges me. I'm all alone. I just need a fucking drink."

"Mom." My whole body was shivering.

"What do you want?" She sneered at me. "Why are you here?"

I stared at her in silence. This was someone I wasn't used to seeing. In all my years, I'd never seen this side of her. This ugly, hateful side. A part of me felt like the numbness I was feeling inside would never leave me.

"You think that just because you have money you can judge me? I see the way you look at me. I see that you think you're better than me, but I'm your mother, do you hear me? I'm the one that brought you into this world. I could have had an abortion, but I chose to keep you. Who do you think you are? Judging me? You're no better than me. You're a piece of trash, you pig. You think I don't know that you're just like your dad. You think I don't know you fuck every piece of pussy you can get. Who are you to fucking judge me? I just want a fucking drink. I'm not hurting anyone."

"You're not hurting anyone?" I jumped up, my face ashen as I stared at her. "You're killing yourself."

"I can do what I Goddamn want." She shook her head. "Do you have any fucking money?"

"What happened to you?" I asked stiffly as I stared at her. "You're not the person I remember from when I was younger. What sort of mother are you?"

"I don't know." Her anger subsided and she collapsed back onto the couch, and looked at the ground. She curled into a ball and started crying. "I just want a drink, please Rhett, I just need a drink."

"Please let me help you, mom." I walked over to her and kneeled on the floor in front of her. "Please let me help you."

"There's nothing you can do." She looked at me with bleak eyes. "I've tried Rhett."

"You can go to rehab again." I said stiffly, my eyes full of unshed tears.

"It doesn't make the pain go away." She shook her head. "It doesn't stop the voices."

"I can help you. I can go with you." I clutched her arm. "Let me help you, mom."

"I'm not your mom." She shook her head and closed her eyes. "I don't deserve to be called your mom."

"Don't you love me mom?"

"I don't even know what love is Rhett." She opened her eyes and stared at me, this time, her eyes were focused on me.

"I'm your son." I whispered and grabbed her hands. "I love you mom, please let me help you."

"I just need a drink." She moaned. "Just one drink."

I dropped her hands and leaned back against the couch and closed my eyes. I stared at the dirty rug in front of me and just sat there. I didn't say anything and neither did she. What was there left to say? What more could I do? There was nothing left. I stared at the walls and saw some photos of myself and Clementine and I wondered why she even had them up.

"Beautiful kids, those two." She pointed at the wall. "My son and his girlfriend. Just beautiful."

"Mom." I turned to her, feeling confused. "That's me."

"Yes, yes." She blinked. "You and Clemmie when you were young."

"I'm surprised you have the photos up."

"You two are like two peas in a pod. Couldn't split you up we couldn't. Your dad was worried of course. He thought you might be...you know."

"No? What?" I frowned.

"Gay."

"What?"

"Your dad thought you might be in the gay way. Seeing as your best friend was a girl."

"I'm not gay." I rolled my eyes.

"I know and he knows. He wouldn't have disowned you. Maybe his parents would have had some issues, but he was fine."

"Okay, well that's good to know."

"I knew you weren't gay though." She smiled sweetly. "The way you looked at that girl and the way she looked at you, I always knew."

"Mom, we were kids."

"You were kids that were in love."

"Mom, we weren't in love as kids."

"You just didn't know." She rubbed my head and for a few seconds, I thought that everything was going to be okay.

"And you did?"

"A mother always knows." She stood up and walked to a photo. It was a shot of Clementine firing water at me from a hose. There was a look of delight on both of our faces and as I stood there staring at the photo, I was transported back to that day. Clementine's hair had been up in some sort of plait and she'd been wearing shorts as she sprayed me, giggling in delight. I'd danced back and forth, trying to jump through the water. It had been a perfect day. A perfect memory.

"Do you remember how much the two of you liked to play Hide N' Seek?" She looked at me for a few seconds.

"Not really." I shook my head.

"Every time I took you both to the park, you'd both want to play Hide N' Seek and you'd always be the one to hide and she'd always be the one to find you."

"The most fun part of the game was hiding." I laughed as I looked at the photos of the two of us. "She could never find me."

"That girl always loved you. She'll love you until the end of days." She looked at me and kissed my cheek. "I'm sorry Rhett."

"Sorry for what?"

"I'm sorry I couldn't be who you wanted me to be." She held me closer to her. "I'm sorry I couldn't be the mother that you needed."

"You still can be."

"I can't." She kissed my cheek. "There are days I don't even recognize myself, Rhett. There are moments I'm so consumed by darkness that I don't even know what to do."

"I can help you." I held her tightly. "That's why I'm here. I can help you."

"I've tried baby. I'm so tired. I just can't, not anymore." She said softly. "It consumes me."

"Try for me mom. Try for me."

"I wish I could."

"I'll get you into rehab. I'll visit you every day. You can do this. Please mom." I pulled back and stared into her eyes, my eyes imploring her to do this, for me, for her son. "Please mom, if you love me, please. Try one last time. Please."

"Do you have any money?" She asked softly, biting down on her lower lip. "I just need one drink. One drink will help me think."

There's a point in your life when all hope for humanity and life is gone. There's a point when you realize that love doesn't fix everything. There's a point where you realize that there is no point to anything. There's a point when the pain feels so deep and so hard that you don't even know how you can keep going on. There's a point where all you want to do is close your eyes and not wake up. There's a point when you realize that you're not enough. That you're never going to be enough. That's a point that kills you inside. That's a point that's a game changer in life. That's a point where a lot of people don't recover. It's so hard to come back from the pits of hell with a positive outlook. It's so hard to lose your heart, your self-esteem, your feelings of peace and comfort. It's so easy to lose yourself. And it's oh so hard to find yourself again. I wish I could tell you that I left her house and went home. I wish I could tell you that I didn't buy a bottle of wine. I wish I could tell you that I didn't love who my mother was when she drank. When she drank she was someone else. She was fun, she was loving, and she was my mom. Until, she had one too many and then she became angry and bitter. I wish I could tell you that I didn't sleep outside in her yard that night, just staring at the stars. I wish I could tell you that I didn't feel like I was in a pit of despair. I wish I could tell you that I didn't wake up the next morning and go and drink some more. I wish I could tell you that I didn't ignore Clementine's calls. I wish I could tell you that I didn't end up going to a bar. I wish I could tell you that I didn't leave the bar with a girl called Victoria. I wish I could tell you all of that.

Eleven

RHETT

Merriam-Webster Dictionary defines sanity as the condition of being based on reason or good judgment. Good judgment is something I've always thought I've had. But then, don't we all think that? Driving back to my house with Victoria was not good judgment. Sitting outside my house in my car with Victoria was not good judgment. Watching Victoria squeeze her breasts was not good judgment. Sitting back and wondering what the fuck I was doing was good judgment. Wanting to punch myself in the face was good judgment. Realizing that I was about to make the biggest mistake of my life was good judgment.

"Are we going inside?" She leaned forward and licked her lips. "I want to see if your cock is as big as your hands."

"What?"

"You know what they say, big hands, big cock." She licked her lips.

"I thought it was big feet?"

"Whatever." She grinned. "Are we going inside or what?"

"No." I shook my head. "I need to take you home."

"What?" She made a face. "Are you fucking joking?"

"Sorry this was a mistake."

"What was a mistake? We haven't even fucked yet."

"I don't want to sleep with you." I stared at her, but all I could think about was Clementine. There was a ringing in my ears and I felt faint. "I'm sorry, but I have to take you home."

"What are you? Some sort of weirdo?"

"Yes, I'm a big weirdo." I started the car again. "Where do you live?"

"Is this some sort of joke?" She looked confused as I started the car. "Are you seriously taking me home?"

"Sorry, I'm just not interested. I wasn't in my right mind." My skin felt hot with shame. What had I been thinking? I could barely remember the last two days. My head was heavy and I felt shame in my heart.

"Just take me to Main and Columbus." She hissed at me. "I'll figure it out from there."

"I can take you home."

"Just take me to Main." She sat back and we drove back into town in silence. She jumped out of the car without a goodbye as I dropped her off. I can't say I blamed her for being upset, but I was more worried about what Clementine was going to say. I knew that she wouldn't be happy with what I'd nearly done. She might even dump me. I hadn't actually cheated, but I knew that the mere fact that I'd taken someone home was bad enough. I felt sick inside. I drove to one of the old country roads, pulled over and called Clementine. The phone rang and rang, but she didn't answer. I tried calling about five times and left a few voicemails, but she didn't pick up or call me back. I got out of the car and stood there for a few minutes before deciding to go for a run. I knew that a run would help to clear the cobwebs from my head.

I ran fast, trying to rid the guilt and pain. I ran, in hopes of forgetting my mother. I ran in hopes of eradicating the deep regret I had. I ran in hopes of becoming a better man. I ran in hopes of finding myself. I ran for what seemed like hours, yet I didn't feel any better when I got back to my car; especially when I saw that Clementine hadn't returned any of my calls. I drove back to my house feeling like a lost, little puppy. I sat in my car outside my house, not even wanting to go inside. I didn't belong here anymore. It didn't feel like home. I closed my eyes and before I knew it, I was falling into a deep uncomfortable sleep.

Knock Knock. The sound of someone knocking on my window awoke me and I jumped. I turned to look at who was outside my car and my heart stopped. There was Clementine. My Clementine. She stood there with wide, caring eyes and a small smile on her face.

"Open up, Rhett." She mouthed and for a second I wasn't sure if I was imagining things. Was she really here? What was she doing here?

"Clementine?" I slowly opened the door and got out as she stepped back.

"Rhett." She surveyed me for a few seconds and then looked back into my eyes.

"Clementine." I said again and then looked away. "What are you doing here?"

"Isn't that my question for you?" She stepped forward. "Why are you sleeping in your car?"

"I called you last night." I said accusingly.

"I was on a plane." She stared back at me. "I've been calling you for the last two days."

"I was busy."

"You saw your mom?"

"Yeah." I shrugged. "Why are you here?"

"It was a mistake to let you come by yourself." She put her arms around me. "I shouldn't have let you come by yourself."

"I'm a big boy. I don't need you coming with me everywhere I go."

"She hurt you?" She touched the side of my hair.

"Who hurt me?"

"What happened with your mom?"

"I can't remember. It doesn't matter."

"She loves you Rhett." She whispered in my ear. "She just doesn't know how to show it."

"She showed me when we got drunk together."

"You drank together."

"Yes." I laughed. "I'm an enabler, didn't you know?"

"Its okay, Rhett. This isn't your fault." She pulled my head towards her. "Look at me."

"Why?" I snapped, staring into her brown eyes. "What's the point?"

"This isn't your fault, Rhett."

"I wanted to help her, yet I was just as bad as her."

"You can't blame yourself for her disease."

"I brought someone home last night." I stared into her eyes. "Victoria was her name. I picked her up in a bar and I brought her home with me." I said bitterly, wanting Clementine to know exactly who I was. I could see the pain and hurt in her eyes and I knew that it was over. Clementine would never want to be with someone like me now.

"What did you do?" She asked me softly, not stepping away from me.

"Nothing." I said after a few seconds. "I didn't do anything. I took her back home. I didn't want to be with her. I didn't want to touch her or kiss her. I just couldn't think straight. I wanted to get rid of the pain. I wanted to just be someone else. I wanted to forget everything."

Clementine eyes were soft, but she just stood there, saying nothing.

"I don't know what to do Clementine. I don't know what to do. I don't know how to deal with this. I don't know how to stop this pain. I don't know what to do."

Still she said nothing. She hugged me tighter and I could feel myself breaking in half. I couldn't lose Clementine. If I lost Clementine, I would have absolutely nothing.

"I'm so sorry Clementine. I'm so sorry. I don't know what to say." I cried into her hair and we just stood there holding each other. The warmth of her body next to mine filled me up with hope. And it also filled me with a calmness I hadn't felt in a long time. "I want to spend my life with you, Clementine."

"Let's go inside." She pulled away from me. "We need to talk." She looked away from me and I could feel my heart dropping. Was this it then? She grabbed my hand and we walked to my front door. "Let's go to your room." She led me through to my bedroom and jumped onto the bed. I sat next to her and gave her a big smile.

"Is this the part where we make love?"

She didn't laugh or smile at me words.

"Bad joke?" I asked again, trying to rid the room of the tension. As I stared at her, I knew that whatever was coming next was going to define our relationship.

"Holden came over last night." She said softly. "We sat on the couch and we watched a movie. He had his arm around my shoulders." She paused. "We didn't do anything though."

"What?" My face was hot and red and there was a huge knot building in my stomach. "He what?" I shouted, the sound of anger filling the room. "How could you do that?" I glared at her. "What the fuck, Clemmie!"

"Holden didn't come over." Clementine sighed. "I wouldn't be that stupid. I just want you to see how it feels. It's not nice is it, Rhett? The thought of someone you love being intimate with someone else, or putting themselves in a position to be intimate."

"Wait, what?" I frowned. "So he didn't go over to watch a movie?"

"No, of course not." She sighed.

"Thank God." I took a deep breath.

"But you did have a girl here with you last night."

"She never came into the house."

"That doesn't make it better." She shook her head. "Plenty of shit can go down in the car."

"I didn't touch her or kiss her, Clemmie."

"That's meant to make me feel better?"

"I wasn't in a good place."

"That doesn't make it better, Rhett." She sighed. "I don't know if I can do this."

"Do what?" I moved closer to her. "What are you saying?"

"I don't know if I can be the—"

"Clementine, stop."

"No, wait." She spoke up. "Let me speak."

"Clementine, please give me a chance to explain."

"No." She shook her head. "Let me speak first." She jumped up off of the bed and paced back and forth. Then she turned to look at me. "I'm so mad at you right now Rhett Madison. I'm so mad at you." She paused and stared at me. "A part of me hates you for what you did. I don't care if you didn't do anything, but there are moments in your life. There are moments in your life that you understand are about more than you. You understand that even if someone hurts you or you feel upset and angry, you can't make it about you. There are moments that are journeys. This is your journey, Rhett. I didn't fully understand. I can't understand. I'm not you. I love you, but I'm not you. I want to be enough. I want to be the one that can fix your pain, but I can't. I can't do that for you and I understand that now. I understand that I can love you until the end of my life with all the love in the world and that won't be enough to heal you. And that doesn't mean that my love isn't enough and it doesn't mean that my love isn't appreciated. It just means that there is more in your life than me. There's more in your heart. This is your journey Rhett and it's a bumpy one. It's one filled with pain and I hate that. But this is your moment. This is your moment to grow. I'm not going to stop that."

"Are you going to leave me?" I asked her softly.

"I could never leave you, Rhett." She shook her head slowly. "I could never leave you. You're a piece of my heart. I will always be here for you. I will always be a shoulder to cry on. I will always be someone you can talk to and joke with. I will always be someone to hold you tight."

"My mom wishes she had an abortion."

"Oh Rhett." She ran towards me. "Oh Rhett."

"She wishes she married someone else. She thinks that she'd have a different life if she had married someone else and had other kids. They would have been enough. Not me though. I'm not enough."

"You know that's not true right? You know she's just trying to hurt you because she's hurt. You know she's displacing her own feelings onto you."

"It hurt, Clementine. I lost myself in that moment. I lost all hope."

"You will always be enough Rhett." She held me to her and grabbed my hand. "You feel my heart beating?" I nodded as I felt the thump thump of her heart against my palm. "That heart pumps with love for you. It has been yours for as long as I can remember. I'm not going to give up on you now."

"So what do we do now?"

"I think you need to see a therapist." She said slowly. "I think you need to learn how to deal with these feelings of rejection. I think you need to go to church."

"Really? Church?" I raised an eyebrow at her.

"Nanna suggested it to me." She nodded. "I know you've got mixed feelings about religion, but you know I think it could help you."

"So you want me to go to church and to see a therapist? Anything else?"

"I think we need to date properly." She looked at me shyly. "I think we rushed into this a bit too fast. I think we need to date. You need to woo me."

"Woo you?" I laughed for the first time that night. "Say what?"

"I want you to take me on dates. I want you to plan special things for us to do. I want you to write me love letters. I want you to show me how much I mean to you."

"What?" I frowned. "You know how I feel about you."

"Rhett."

"Fine." I shook my head. "I'll woo you." I laughed. "Anything else? Or shouldn't I ask?"

"I don't think we should live together."

"Are you out of your mind?" I glared at her. "Are you out of your mind, Clementine O'Hara?"

"No." She shook her head slightly.

"I'm not moving out." I shook my head. "Hell no."

"What?"

"I love you, Clementine. I will do anything you ask, but I'm not moving out. No way, Jose. The best part of my day is waking up with you."

"We can still wake up together."

"So what's the point of different apartments if we're spending every night together anyway?"

"I just thought..."

"You thought or someone else thought and suggested that?"

"Rhett." She groaned.

"Answer me this, Clemmie. Do you really want to live apart?" I stared into her eyes, my heart beating fast. I knew I would honor her request if she said yes.

"No." She sighed. "I love living with you, even though you make a mess and blame it on me."

"I love living with you as well." I laughed. "That settles it. I'm not moving out."

"So..." Her voice trailed off and I leaned down and kissed her.

"Thank you for coming back for me. Thank you for loving me." I whispered against her lips.

"I couldn't not come, Rhett. I could feel your pain as real as if I were there." She kissed me back, her fingers running to my hair.

"I'm not going to let you face this alone. I'm not going to let your mom break your heart and leave you all alone. I know it hurts. I know you don't understand, but sometimes there are things we will never understand. There are pains we will never be able to fix. That doesn't mean we give up. That doesn't mean we don't continue. Those questions may never leave you Rhett. You may never understand why your mom is like that, but it's not because of you. It's not because you're not enough. It's never because of that Rhett. It's never because of that."

RHETT
TWO MONTHS LATER

There are days when everything seems okay and I forget that I'm a man with a mom that didn't love him enough. There are days when I feel like I'm flying I'm so happy. And then there are days that the darkness of my thoughts scare me. The hollowness in my heart makes me feel incomplete. However there's something funny about life. No matter how bad you feel for yourself, there is always another moment of happiness to embrace.

"Rhett, come here." Clementine screamed at me from the bathroom.

"I'm coming." I groaned as I got up from the couch. "You do know that I'm watching football right and the—"

"Rhett, this is important." She screamed again and my heart stopped. Oh shit, was Clementine pregnant? They say that time stands still when you find out you're having a baby. I have to admit that time wasn't standing out as I ran to the bathroom. My heart was beating fast and all I could think about was, am I going to be a dad?

"Rhett, don't come in yet." Clementine shouted as I pushed the bathroom door open. "I need a second."

"It's okay, Clemmie. I'll be here for you. You know I'm not going anywhere."

"You might change your mind." She cried out and I froze. So it was true. She was pregnant. I felt a glimmer of excitement and fear.

"It's okay, Clemmie. We both engaged in the sex, we can both take care of the baby."

"Baby?" Clementine flung the door open. "What baby?" She looked at me in confusion as I stared back at her in shock.

"Whoa what happened to you?" I couldn't stop myself from laughing at her bright pink hair.

"I was just trying to dye my hair red." She groaned. "I don't know what happened."

"But your hair is pink."

"I know that." She wailed. "Don't laugh at me." She made a face.

"Is this why you called me?" I looked into her face. "Because of your hair?"

"Yes, because of my hair. I look a hot mess."

"You're not pregnant?"

"Pregnant?" She blushed. "No. Why would you think that?"

"Well, there have been quite a few occasions that we didn't use protection."

"Rhett." She made a face at me.

"What?" I laughed. "Okay, I know it's not funny, but it's true. It wouldn't be a huge shock if you ended up pregnant."

"Rhett, my hair." She held it in her hands. "What am I going to do?"

"Clementine, I have no idea." I shook my head, bent down, gave her a quick kiss and walked back to the living room. "Sorry, but I'm missing the game."

"You suck."

"Sorry, if it was about a baby I'd still be there." I shouted. "You know I love you, but I can't do much to help you pink lady."

"Well I have pink hair and I'm pregnant." She cried out and I jumped up again in shock.

"What?" I ran to the bathroom again. "You're pregnant."

"No goofy." She laughed and then paused. "At least I don't think I am."

"Stop punking me."

"Why? It's so much fun."

"I'm going to pick you up and carry you outside and dump you in the snow."

"You better not." She poked me in the chest.

"Why not, you'd look hot as a snowman with pink hair." I laughed. "Remember when we used to make snow angels?"

"Yeah." She nodded. "That was fun, but we were also kids."

"We were teenagers." I grabbed her hand and pulled her towards me. "And I'm sure you could still have fun doing it, even though you're a crusty old woman."

"You're a crusty old man."

"We're the crusties." I pulled her in the bedroom to dance with me. "Hey hey, we're the crusties."

"And people say we crusty around." She sang along with me as I spun her around the room, giggling.

"But we're too busy dying our hair pink to let anybody down."

"You're mean."

"Who me? Couldn't be."

"Go and watch your football, Rhett." She groaned. "Go and watch football and let me deal with my crusty pink hair."

"It's not crusty, it's cute."

"It's not cute." She made a face at me. "Go and watch football."

"I'm sorry you don't like your hair." I pulled her to the bed to lay with me.

"It's fine." She pouted. "I'll deal with it."

"I have something I want you to watch when you have time."

"Oh?" She made a face. "You know I'm not really into football."

"It's not football." I smiled.

"What is it?"

"You have to come and see."

"I don't want to watch football."

"I just told you, it's not football."

"Okay."

"Come." I grabbed her hand and took a deep breath as we walked to the living room. "I wanted to do this right."

"Do what right?"

"Just watch this video and I'm going to sing you a song."

"You're going to sing me a song?"

"Well, I'm not going to sing it."

"What?" She frowned. "You're confusing me."

"So you know how you love David Berkeley?"

"Uh huh."

"Well you know how I know you love David Berkeley?"

"Uh huh? Where are you going with this Rhett?"

"Just come." I grinned. "Come, sit and listen."

"Okay." She walked with me to the living room and sat down.

I turned the TV on to YouTube and played the video I'd spent the last two weeks making for her. And sang along to the music in the video.

"Look into my eyes girl, and I won't look away

I'll be right beside you till my dying day

Yes it took me a long time, don't know why I was blind

Searched the whole world over, but it was you I was trying to find

Oh won't you be my princess and let me be your knight

I'll love you like in the old days, I swear I'll treat you right

I've been writing you letters. If only in my mind

There ain't no words as pretty as you my Clementine

Oh, now my heart's on fire, it's true

Lay your hand in mine

I want to spend my life with you,

Clementine.

Clementine.

I like the spring in New England, I like the leaves in the fall

But waking up beside you, well I like that most of all

Now it seems so simple, now it feels so right...

Girl you make the sun rise, light up the moon at night

Oh, yeah my heart's on fire, it's true
You fill my mind
I want to spend my life with you,
Clementine
Clementine.
When I look in those brown eyes, I see down the road
Build a home together, make a family of our own
So Clementine O'Hara, I hope that now you see
There's nothing I wouldn't give you, I'm down upon my knee
Oh now my heart's on fire, it's true
The stars align
I want to spend my life with you, Clementine
Clementine.
Clementine be mine."

I watched Clementine's face as she watched all the old videos of us from our childhood. When the video was finished she turned towards me with a look of excitement in her eyes, I got down on one knee and pulled a ring out of my pocket and took a deep breath.

"David Berkeley wrote that song for you, for us." My voice was wobbly. "I know he's your favorite singer and I wanted this moment to be full of all your favorites." I stared into her warm chestnut brown eyes. "I can still remember the first day you spoke to me, I can remember the first smile you gave me, I can remember the first time you tickled me. I can remember the first time you cried with me. I can remember the first time you cried because of me. I can remember the first time you tried to put makeup on. I can remember the first time my heart skipped a beat, you were wearing that yellow dress." I grinned at her. "You had brown hair then, not pink." My heart thudded as I spoke to her and she gave me her sweet smile, her eyes expressing her shock and surprise. "I love you, Clementine. I love you so much that it should be illegal. I love you more than all the stars in the sky. You've made me feel like me again. You've made me feel whole. You've made me realize just how lucky and blessed I am. Marry me Clementine, say you'll marry me and be mine forever. Say you'll be my wife." I grabbed her left hand and licked my lips nervously. "I love you, Clementine O'Hara, will you do me the honor of being my wife?"

"Oh Rhett." She burst into tears and it was my turn to be in shock.

"Oh no, did I upset you?"

"No, I'm just so happy." She gulped.

"So happy that you're going to say yes?"

"Yes." She nodded and laughed. "I'm so happy that I'm going to say yes." I slipped the ring on her finger quickly and then stood up and pulled her up into my arms.

"This is Nanna's ring." I smiled at her. "She wanted you to have it."

"How did she know you were going to propose?"

"I asked your mom and dad for their permission."

"You did not." Her jaw dropped.

"I did." I nodded. "When I went down to see my mom last month." I grinned at her. "Not only did I take my mom to her new rehab facility, but I also spent time with your parents. Jake even came up for a day."

"I can't believe you didn't tell me."

"And ruin the surprise?"

"But I..."

"Clemmie, I've been dying to tell you for over a month." I laughed as I held her close to me. "This wasn't even how I planned on proposing."

"It wasn't?"

"No, but when I saw your hot pink hair and I thought about us having a baby, I knew I couldn't not ask you right now. This is the moment. This is our moment. It's crazy. It's weird. It's funny. It's full of love. It's perfect for us."

"Did you think we'd ever be here?" She kissed me on the lips.

"In a living room in Boston kissing?" I cocked my head. "Nope."

"No silly. Here, as in, engaged and in love?"

"I don't know whether I should answer that." I bit my lower lip. "I don't know if you want to hear the answer to that question."

"It's okay if you didn't." She stroked my face. "I know you used to be a man-whore."

"Oh, how little you know." I pulled her down to the couch with me. "When I was fourteen years old I had a dream that you were my wife."

"What?" She shrieked. "No you didn't."

"Yes I did." I smiled at her smugly.

"You never told me."

"Of course I didn't tell you. I was freaked out." I laughed. "I did not want to be having dreams of marrying my best friend."

"Oh of course not."

"Not because I didn't think you were the prettiest girl in the class." I clasped her hands to my heart. "You've always been the most beautiful girl I know. I was always worried that if we did anything, I'd lose you. I'd lose my best friend and nothing was worth that."

"You know you'll never lose me."

"That's why I'm marrying you." My hand found her breast. "I want you to be mine forever and I want everyone in the world to know. You will be Clementine Madison and you will be my wife."

"And here I thought you wanted me for my brains."

"I want you for your brains because I want us to have intelligent kids. I also want you for the love and compassion you have towards me. I also want you for the kindness you have shown my mother and I during the last couple of months and the fact that you come to my therapy sessions with me. You've made me see that everything in my life doesn't have to be perfect. It's okay to feel pain. It's okay to be upset. It's okay to be disappointed. You've made me realize that there's nothing lacking in me because my mother has issues. Those are her issues and I can love her and support her, but she makes her decisions and they have nothing to do with me. You've made me realize how selfless love truly is. You've made me realize that when one truly loves, there is nothing that anyone can say or do to stop that love."

"We're really lucky, Rhett." She held my head in her hands. "We're really and truly lucky to have found each other. I never would have believed it if I hadn't seen it with my own two eyes."

"Believed what?" I asked confused.

"I never would have believed that I'd see you, Rhett, in love."

"Get used to it Clemmie because I, Rhett Madison am more in love with you than anyone has ever been with anyone before. And my love for you grows and grows. I love you so much Clementine. And that's something that is never going to change."

THE END

WATCH THE ENGAGEMENT VIDEO THAT RHETT MADE FOR CLEMENTINE HERE: HTTP://JSCOOPERAUTHOR.COM/RHETT-IN-LOVE-ENGAGEMENT-MOVIE/

THE END

NOTE FROM THE AUTHOR:

I hope you enjoyed Rhett in Love. This was a very special book to me and I hope you enjoyed the interactive part of the book. Please leave a review if you enjoyed Rhett in Love.
Please join my mailing list (http://jscooperauthor.coom/mailing-list/) to be notified of all my new books and to read upcoming teasers.

BOOKS CURRENTLY AVAILABLE FOR PREORDER

Illusion
If Only Once (The Martelli Brother's)
One Night Stand
To You, From Me
Books available to read now
Finding My Prince Charming
The Last Boyfriend
Scarred
Everlasting Sin
The Ex Games
Rhett
Crazy Beautiful Love

EXCLUSIVE TEASER FROM ILLUSION

PROLOGUE

"Bianca, where are you?" His voice sounded angry, and I shivered as I opened my eyes.

I stared at the large expanse of blue sky through the tree branches and prayed that he didn't find me. I could see the white-sand beaches from my vantage point. The whole island looked so much smaller from up here. My limbs felt numb, but I was too scared to even move an inch. If he heard the rustling of leaves, he'd know where I was. I closed my eyes again and tried not to think about falling.

"Bianca, this isn't funny." His voice was hoarse, and I heard his footsteps moving closer to me. "Bianca, if you can hear me . . ." He paused, and his voice changed. "Please don't make this harder than it has to be. I'm not going to hurt you."

I heard a branch snap below me, and I knew he was close. All he had to do was look up. If he looked up, he'd be able to find me. This man who'd become my most intimate confidante was now my predator, and I was his prey. I opened my eyes and took a deep breath before looking down. An involuntary gasp escaped my mouth as I realized how high up I was. That was my first mistake.

"I've found you," he whispered as he looked up at me with dark eyes. "When will you learn? You can't escape me."

"Did you hurt him?" My fingers started trembling as I looked back down at him. "Tell me. Did you hurt him?"

"It depends on what you mean by hurt." He lifted his hands up, and I saw that his fingers were drenched in blood.

I closed my eyes; I had my answer.

"I did it for us," he said simply, and I felt my heart drop into my stomach. "Don't you trust me?" he asked me softly as he started to climb the tree. I saw the shiny glitter of the silver knife in his left hand before he placed it into his pocket and my heart stopped beating for a second.

"I trust you." I nodded and waited for him to reach me.

That was my second mistake.

PROLOGUE

ONE WEEK EARLIER

"Can I have this seat?" A deep voice interrupted my typing and I stifled a sigh.

"Uh, sure." I replied without looking up. I had to finish my latest movie review in the next ten minutes and email it to my editor if I wanted to get paid for the article.

"Can I have some space on the table?" His voice was dry as he spoke again and I pulled my laptop towards me quickly, my eyes never leaving my screen. "I don't mean to disturb you." He continued and this time I ignored him completely. I didn't have time for chitchat. Not when I had to find to finish an article on Adam Sandler's latest movie and convince viewers to go and watch it without completely lying about my feelings towards the acting and the poor jokes.

I typed away as quickly as I could, but I could feel that the man was staring at me. I bit down on my lower lip to stop myself from looking up at him and asking what his problem was? It wasn't his fault that I was on high alert and anxious. I knew that I couldn't have an expectation of privacy if I was working at a coffee shop, but I didn't normally have to worry about a stranger talking to me. People in New York never talked to strangers, not unless they were tourists.

I sighed and looked up, "did you need help with something?" My breath caught as I stared at the man's face. He was handsome, or appeared to be under the Yankees cap that covered half of his forehead. His blue eyes looked into mine with a bright light and I could see a hint of a smile on his full pink lips. I licked my lips unconsciously as I stared at the man across from me and attempted to brush my messy hair back.

"No, you've done enough. Thank you." He nodded and looked down at his book in a dismissive fashion. Served me right, I suppose. I hadn't really given him the time of day and it would be way too obvious if I tried to start up a conversation now. I looked at my watch and then back at my article, I had five minutes to sum up a lackluster review of a movie I'd thought was inane. If I didn't send it over, I wouldn't get paid. And now that this was my only form of income, I needed to get paid. I went back to typing, though my mind was partially on the man I was sharing the table with. His knee was rubbing against mine and I couldn't help but laugh at myself for the slight thrill his touch was giving me.

"Loser," I whispered to myself under my breath as I wrapped up the article and attached it in an email. I knew that I was sending the email without rereading the article one more time so that I could try and chat to the man. Though, I really had no business trying to flirt with a strange man in a coffee shop. I was about to ask him what he was reading when I got the strangest sensation that someone was watching me again. And this time I knew it wasn't the man sharing the table with me. I looked around the coffee shop and saw an older looking man sipping his coffee and staring at me over a newspaper. As soon as our eyes made contact, he looked away and back down at his paper. I felt my heart racing as I stared at his coffee cup on the table. It wasn't from this coffee shop. I pressed send on my email and grabbed my bag up from the floor in a panic, spilling half of its contents on the ground.

"You need some help?" The man looked up from his book and stared at the ground. He leaned down and picked up my lipstick and some mints and handed them to me. Our fingers brushed each other as I took my belongings from him and I felt a dart of electricity running through me at his touch.

"Thanks." I stared into his deep blue eyes and nodded quickly.

"Is everything okay?" His eyes crinkled in concern and I was about to answer when I felt the man in the corner staring at me again.

"I think I'm being followed." I said as I shook my head and jumped up. "Sorry, I have to go." I grabbed my laptop and pushed it into my bag. "It was nice meeting you." I gave him a quick smile and ran out of the coffee shop. I continued running down the street until I could no longer run anymore. I stopped outside a donut shop and leaned back against the wall, breathing deeply. I looked left and right to make sure I didn't see the man that I was pretty sure had been following me and then rubbed my forehead.

"You're going crazy, Bianca." I muttered to myself as I straightened up and started walking at a normal pace. I started laughing as I reached the subway station and went down to catch my train. Not one person had looked at me like I was crazy as I'd run down the street like I was in the 100m sprint finals at the Olympics. That was part of the beauty to living in the City. You could be who you wanted and you weren't judged. The other side of the coin, the side of the equation that made me stop smiling was the wonder of what would have happened, if the man had been following me. Would anyone have come to my aid? I walked onto the subway and held onto the rails without looking at anyone. As I stood there I thought about both men in the coffee shop, one that I'd wanted to get to know better and the other that I hoped I never saw again. I shook my head as I realized how different I was now. My life had changed completely and so had I.

I NEVER THOUGHT I was particularly brave until recently. I don't enjoy watching horror movies. I sleep with all my doors double-locked and I go through and check all my windows are closed tight every night before I go to bed; and I live on the eighth floor of my apartment building. No, I'm not someone that anyone would call brave and definitely not an amateur sleuth. I've always been someone that likes to keep to herself. Some people would call be quiet, but those are the ones that don't know me well. Inside I'm a dynamo of activity and fun.

I used to be the sort of person that froze when she heard a creak in the floorboards or heard a sudden scream. My father always used to call me his little frightened rabbit when I was growing up. I heard the term a lot as there were always sudden and unexplainable noises in New York City. I don't think he realized that it was his overprotectiveness that led to my lack of trust of most people. However, my whole demeanor changed when my father died.

My father died of a broken heart. Or rather I should say he died with a broken heart. I don't think he ever got over my mother's death. I'm not sure that I ever got over it either, even though I was a young girl when she passed away in a car accident. Her English ancestry was the reason I studied British history in college and my love of her memory was the reason why when I found my father's secret box, I knew I had to do something about its contents. My mother's death changed my father's life and my father's death changed mine. The moment I read his letter to me was the moment I felt steel implanted in my backbone. It was the moment I knew that I wouldn't allow anything to frighten me until I found out what had really happened to my mother.

I WASN'T SURPRISED when the letter arrived. It was only after I read the note that I looked back at the envelope for clues. Only then did I realize there was no postal stamp. Whoever had left the note for me didn't want any clues leading back to them. I stared at the letter in my hands and shivered slightly. It read simply:

Beauty and Charm. One survives. One is destroyed. What are your odds?

I read it again, trying to make sense of the note. I wasn't sure what I was supposed to take from it. I picked up the envelope again to see if there was anything inside that I'd missed. While I hadn't been surprised to receive the letter, I had been surprised by its contents. I hadn't expected such a blatant threat, though it shouldn't have surprised me. My father had warned me in the letter I'd found in his box, that there were people willing to do anything to keep their secrets safe. His letter had stated that he suspected that my mother's car accident hadn't really been an accident. However, his suspicions had come too late. It was only on his deathbed, that he had started to remember conversations and actions that had happened previous to her death. His letter spoke of his sadness and regret at having shutdown after my mothers death. He felt that if he'd not been in such a deep state of depression, that he would have made the connections earlier. His letter didn't directly ask me to find out the truth, but I could read between the lines. He wanted justice for my mother. It was the reason why he'd written the letter in the first place. The only problem was, my father didn't say whom he suspected. All he had left me was a one-page letter, talking of his suspicions and a box full of paperwork from the corporation he'd used to work for, Bradley Inc.

After I'd read my father's letter and gone through the paperwork he'd left for me, I had started investigating. Well, I'd done my best to get on the inside of Bradley, Inc., so that I could find clues that might help me figure out what my father had found out and if my mother had been murdered. I hadn't been careful enough with my investigation and so I wasn't surprised that I had been contacted. Though, I was taken aback by the letter. Frankly, it wasn't what I'd expected to receive.

I stared at the letter in my hands again and frowned. There was a veiled threat and a challenge in the note. "One survives and one is destroyed." Destroyed was a pretty powerful word. Destroyed was sending a message. I could feel my fingers trembling as they held the letter. I knew that I was getting close to the truth. To the answers that would prove my father's suspicions had been correct. I was about to take out a pen and paper and write down the words

I thought were most telling in the note when I heard a loud banging on the apartment door.

"Open up!" a masculine voice shouted as he banged. "Police."

Police? I walked to the door with a perplexed expression. "I'm coming!" I called out as I opened the door. I felt a little taken aback that someone had made it into the building without calling up. How had he gotten into the building without someone buzzing him in? I dismissed my thoughts as I realized the police must have master keys to every building in the city, though I still felt some discomfort as I looked at him,

"Are you okay?" The policeman had his hand on his gun in its holster, and I swallowed.

"I'm fine. What's going on?"

"There was a nine-one-one call from your apartment." He pushed past me. "And then a hang-up."

"I didn't make a nine-one-one call." I shook my head and pulled my cell phone out of my pocket. "Look, you can check my calls. There is no call to nine-one-one."

"It was made from your landline, ma'am."

"I don't have a landline." I frowned and followed him around my apartment. My voice rose as I wondered who had called nine-one-one on me. "There must have been a mistake. I can assure you that I didn't call nine-one-one and hang up."

"I'm still going to check through your apartment, if that's okay?" He didn't wait for an answer.

"I already told you that I didn't call the police, and I'm the only one who lives here." I called after him and watched as he walked into my bedroom. I stood still, unable to move as I thought back to the letter that had just arrived. Had the writer of the letter sent the police to my house? And if so, why? Why would the people who killed my mother want the police involved in the matter? It didn't make sense. I chewed on my lower lip, deep in thought, when I heard a slamming. "What's going on?" I walked to my bedroom quickly, my heart pounding. "What are you doing in my room?" My voice was jittery and I tried not to look in the one place I was scared he would find.

"I was just making sure that no one was in your closets mam. It doesn't hurt for me to make sure everything is okay." He walked out of my room with a slight frown. "All looks clear."

"I already told you that."

"You have any issues, you call us." His eyes searched mine as he spoke and then he handed me a card. "You can't be too careful these days."

"I'm very careful." I walked him to the door and wondered if I should tell him about the note I'd just received. I was about to when I realized what my father had always told me when I was growing up. "The pockets of the rich are deep. Bianca only trust someone if they give you reason to trust them. Even the police aren't above being bribed." "Thank you for your concern, Officer." I nodded at him and waited for him to leave. My heart was pounding and I needed to think.

"No worries. Stay safe, Ms. London." He nodded his head, and I closed the door. It was only after he left that I realized he knew my name. How had he known my name?

I leaned against the door and closed my eyes. What was going on here? Today was turning into one mysterious day. First the note, and then the police showing up. I didn't know: who sent the note, why the sent the note, who called the police, how he had gotten into my building, and how he knew my name. I chewed my bottom lip as I tried to figure out what was going on. I stared around my apartment and suddenly the coziness of the room felt claustrophobic. I'd always loved living in New York City, but today my small one-bedroom felt like a cell. The building that had seemed so safe when I moved in, suddenly made me feel like a fallacy. I didn't know my neighbors and I had no one to talk to about how the policeman had gotten into the building or the mysterious letter that had arrived.

The dirty peeling walls directly opposite seemed to be closing in on me as I stood there hoping for clarity to hit and questions to be answered miraculously. I walked to my tan leather couch and sat down, leaning back into the plushness of the cushions. It was the only nice piece of furniture I owned. And even then it had been a gift from my best friend, Rosie. I could barely afford the rent in my apartment as it was and I wasn't living in Trump Towers either.

I picked up the bright red and orange patterned cushions that my father had gotten me in India when I was a teenager and then froze as my cellphone rang. The noise was jarring in my eerily quiet living room. I normally always had the TV on or music playing; I didn't like being in quiet spaces for too long. It reminded me of how alone I was. I grabbed my cell phone and dropped it as I stared at the screen. My father's phone number flashed on the screen. My *dead* father's phone number. I stared at it for another second, before reaching down and picking it up again.

"Hello?" I answered softly, my voice cracking as I wondered who was calling me from my dad's phone. I was pretty sure I still had it in a box in my bedroom. I took a deep breath to stop myself from freaking out and jumped off of the couch. "Hello," I spoke into the phone again with my voice trembling, this time I unable to hide how freaked out I was by the call.

"You should be more careful, Bianca," a deep male voice spoke into the phone. I couldn't make his voice out clearly, as the phone had a lot of static.

My voice rose. "Who is this?"

"You shouldn't let strangers into your apartment."

"I haven't let any strangers into my apartment."

"Anyone can be anyone. Haven't you figured that out yet?"

"What are you talking about?" My face started to feel hot as I sat there in fear.

"Be careful of those who seek to help you. They may do more harm than good." Then he hung up.

I stared at the phone in my hand and ran to my bedroom to find my dad's phone. The box of my father's things was on the bed and the lid was off. I ran over to it and saw that the phone was gone. Who could have taken it? No one had been in my apartment in weeks. No one except the policeman, but why would a policeman go through my things? Unless he hadn't been there to help protect me from an intruder as opposed to finding something to protect someone else.

I looked down at the business card he had given me and froze. It was blank. All he had given me was a piece of white card stock. It was then that I knew this was the next step in whatever was going on. I knew then that the policeman had been looking for my father's papers. The papers that he'd left me were full of clues. It didn't matter that I didn't fully understand them yet. Obviously someone else wanted them.

I walked to the window in my living room and looked down to the street. I stared at the homeless woman who'd settled into the block directly across the street a couple of weeks ago. The woman I gave a couple of dollars to once a week as I passed by her. The woman who quoted a different Bible verse to me every time she saw me. The woman who shivered even when the days were warm. The woman who wore a Cartier watch and had freshly dyed highlights. The woman who knew exactly when I left and entered the building. I didn't know who she was, friend or foe, but I knew that she was watching me.

I walked back to my bedroom and stared at my father's box for a few minutes before closing it carefully and placing it back in my closet. I was grateful that I had removed my father's papers from the box several weeks ago. I hadn't known why at the time, but I'm someone that always listens to her first instincts. I then went to my dirty-clothes basket, pulled out my clothes, and threw them onto the floor. I instinctively looked around the room again to make sure it was empty, even though I knew there was no one in there with me. I pulled out my mother's old cedar jewelry box that I'd hidden under the clothes and slowly opened it. I let out a huge breath when I saw the stack of papers hidden under the cheap costume necklaces I had bought at Goodwill. I carefully closed it again, carried it with me to the kitchen, and placed it in a plastic bag. Then I pulled my cell phone out again and made a call.

IT HAD BEEN four days since the note arrived. Four days that I'd been on tenterhooks wondering what was going to happen next. I'd never felt this anxious before. Or scared. However, I tried to continue living my life as I normally did. There was nothing I could do but wait and see what was going to happen next. I also knew what the next step of the plan was. I could do nothing but wait for my ex-boyfriend David to come through for me. He was my only access to more information. I hadn't wanted to trust him, but I knew that in a game of cat and mouse, the one that got the cheese was the one that took the most risks. I just had to be patient. Though, it was hard. Even watching shows on The History Channel didn't capture my attention for long.

"I'm not dating online again," I muttered as I deleted another rude message from a man known as Matt, or as his profile said, KnightInShiningArmani.

Online dating was something I'd been doing since David and I had broken up. At first, it had taken my mind off everything that had gone down with David. Now, it helped me to occupy my thoughts when they drifted to dark areas. Generally, I enjoyed my online conversations, but there was something about Matt that had really turned me off. He just wasn't getting the hint. I'd made the mistake of talking to him twice on the phone before deciding that I wasn't interested in going on a date with him. He definitely looked handsome in his photos, but he'd been arrogant and demanding on the phone, and his e-mails had gotten creepier and creepier. I stifled a sigh as I saw another e-mail come through from Matt and picked up my phone to call my best friend, Rosie.

"This is Rosie speaking." Rosie's voice sounded tired as she answered the phone.

"Hey, it's Bianca." I said lightly and walked over to my vanity. "What are you up to?"

"Just a little something called work," she responded with a sigh. I could tell she was tired from the lack of excitement in her tone. "What's up?"

"Want to grab a drink tonight?" I checked my reflection in the mirror and sighed. Months of facial exercises hadn't helped to define my cheekbones at all. "Not that I need any alcohol. My face looks puffy. However, I haven't seen you in over a month, and we need to catch up. There's some stuff I need to tell you about."

"I'm sure it doesn't look puffy, and yes, we need to catch up." Her tone changed. "I want to hear what you've been up to."

"Trust me, it does," I muttered, frowning at the bags under my eyes. "I'm going to make myself a face mask and put some cucumbers on my eyes."

"Must be nice to be self-employed," Rosie said jealously.

"Must be nice to have a steady income," I responded back tartly. I'd been freelancing writing entertainment articles for a couple of online newspapers for about a year and I wasn't sure if I'd made the right decision. As much as I loved movies, my true love was to the Kings and Queens of England, and I really wanted to become a history professor. However, freelancing gave me the opportunity to act as Sherlock Holmes, or realistically more like Stephanie Plum. I needed the flexibility in my schedule to allow me to investigate what had happened to my mother more freely.

"Touché." She giggled. "And yes. I'm down for a drink. It's been a long month and an even longer day."

"Boss back?" I made small talk even though I didn't want to. I really just wanted to tell her about the note and the fake policeman. I wanted to tell her about the woman who watched me from across the street and the feeling I had that someone was following me. I knew this wasn't the time though. I'd have time to tell her everything tonight.

"Yes, he's back from Shanghai, and he's acting like a bigger douche than ever," she moaned. "He's treating me like his assistant again. It's not like I've been running the department for the last month or anything."

"Drinks are on me, then," I offered. "Maybe he's treating you like that because he knows you can take over his job and do a better one in a heartbeat."

"Bianca, you think very highly of me." She said appreciatively. "However, you can't afford to buy me all the drinks I'm going to need tonight." She laughed and then paused. "Ooh, you also have to tell me how your date went with that guy you met online."

"Oh, I told you about that?" I frowned into the phone, confused. I couldn't remember mentioning that I was going to meet Matt, but ever since I'd started doing detective work on the side, I couldn't really remember who I was telling what. I really needed to keep a journal of the information I was giving to different people. Rosie had been my best friend for years, but I knew that she wouldn't approve of my investigations, so I hadn't really told her much. Though, I was starting to think I needed to confide in her when I saw her later.

"Yeah, you told me you were going to meet that guy online, to help get over David, remember?"

"Oh, that was weeks ago, and I canceled it." I groaned. "I had a feeling that it wasn't going to work out." I stared into my eyes as I spoke, I felt bad about keeping secrets from Rosie.

"Bianca, you can't cancel the date before you meet him. Plus, he looked hot in those photos you showed me online. All masculine and sexy."

"Yeah, he was hot." I nodded as I walked back to my computer. I shook my head as I sat down. I'd obviously told her about Matt if I'd shown her photos. "He just seemed like a bit of a creep."

"They're all creeps." She sounded annoyed. "Anyways, he looked cute."

"I don't want to date a guy who's creepy before we even meet."

"How was he being creepy?"

"Listen to this e-mail he sent me last night." I sat on the bed and put my laptop on my knees. "Hold on a sec. I'm going through my trash, since I deleted the e-mails."

"No worries." She paused. "Hey, I wanted to tell you that I saw David a couple of weeks ago."

"Oh?" My heart stopped for a second, and I took a deep breath. "How did he look?"

"Handsome as ever." She paused again. "Sorry."

"It's fine," I said stiffly as an image of David crossed my mind.

I didn't want to talk about David. Not over the phone. Not now. He was the most handsome guy I'd ever dated, with his dark brown locks and bright green eyes. He was tall and buff, and he looked like every woman's dream. Rosie had been shocked when he'd asked me out and we'd started dating. She hadn't known the lengths I'd gone through to get his attention. Though to be honest, I'd never felt secure in the relationship, and when he'd cheated on me, I hadn't been that surprised. Our relationship had been complex and no one else knew exactly how complex it still was.

"Have you spoken to him recently?"

"Not since we broke up." I bit my lower lip, hating to lie again. "I've started several e-mails though."

"Does he still call you?"

"He called me a few times, but nothing in over a month." I sighed. "Maybe he's moved on."

"He's a dick, and you know what he was thinking with." Rosie sounded hesitant. "I mean, I know guys have needs, but shit, he should have told you that he couldn't wait anymore."

"It wasn't that I didn't want to sleep with him." I sighed. "It just never felt right. I wanted it to be special." And it would never have been special with David, no matter how handsome I thought he was.

"I know. He's an asshole." Rosie went back to being supportive. "It's his loss."

"Exactly." I sighed as I thought back to David. "Did he say anything to you when you saw him?" I asked casually.

"He said hi." Rosie's voice sounded awkward. "And something else, but it didn't make sense."

"Oh?" My fingers froze on the keyboard. "What else did he say?"

"He said that there was more than one way to skin a cat."

"What?" I frowned. "What does that mean?"

"I don't know. I've been thinking about it a lot. I think he's trying to woo you." Rosie's voice became thoughtful. "I guess he figured out that just apologizing and calling wasn't going to cut it. I bet he's going to try to step it up a notch and really try harder to win you back."

"You think so?" I stared around my bedroom and thought for a second. This was the one room in my apartment that David and I had never really spent much time in. I lay back on my bed and sighed. "I was an idiot, wasn't I? I should have just had sex with him. I'm sure it would have been amazing. Maybe we'd still be together now." I felt odd saying the words, as if I were playing a part in a play. *You've been watching too many movies, Bianca*, I thought to myself.

"Don't blame yourself, Bianca. It's not your fault. Maybe this is what he needed, to see how much you mean to him. Maybe he'll be all romantic now. What if he takes you on a surprise trip to Paris or something? Wouldn't that be cool?"

"You think he'd really do that?"

"Who knows?" Rosie laughed. "Hey, hold on. I just got a package from a new and very cute delivery guy."

"Okay." I laughed and sat back up, still looking through my e-mails for the deleted messages from Matt. I wanted to get away from the conversation about David.

I should have known that he was going to be an asshole from his screen name. I mean, Knight in Shining Armani? Only a pompous asshole would choose such a name.

"Thank you, Billy." I heard Rosie speaking to the delivery guy and ripping open her new package.

I smiled to myself as I imagined her decimating the package so she could find out what was inside as quickly as possible. She'd always been impatient when opening packages and presents. I only hoped she treated any packages she received from me with more care. I stared at the plastic bag on my night desk and wondered if I was making the right decision to entrust my papers with her.

"Oh my God, are you there, Bianca?" Rosie's voice was jittery and excited.

"Yeah, why?"

"Someone just sent me a present."

"Ooh, what did they send?"

"A Tiffany's bracelet and a note." Her voice was growing louder with excitement.

"What does it say?" I asked casually as my stomach flip-flopped.

"It says, 'my dearest Rosie, you don't know me yet, but I very much want to know you. Accept this gift as a token of my friendship.'" She paused. "And that's it."

"Who's it from?"

"I don't know." Her voice was low. "I wonder if it's Joe from accounting. I've seen him giving me a few rather obvious admiring stares recently, ever since I got those blond highlights."

"But you know Joe. Wouldn't it say, 'You don't know my intentions yet' as opposed to 'You don't know me yet'?"

"Who knows? Maybe he's slow or didn't think it through properly." She laughed. "Who cares? I just got a bracelet from Tiffany's."

"I can't wait to see it tonight." I was slightly envious. No one was sending me gifts from Tiffany's. Not even David, who might or might not be trying to woo me back. I thought back to my own, more ominous note and wondered if there was a connection.

"I can't wait to show it off." Rosie's squeal interrupted my thoughts.

"Okay, I have the e-mails open. Are you ready to hear the craziness?"

"Yes, let me hear."

"'Dear CreativeGirlNYC, Have you ever been to Rome? It's such a romantic city that I would love to fly you there in my private jet. I'd like to take you to the Trevi Fountain and Spanish Steps. Then we can share pasta and drink wine as we gaze into each other's eyes. KnightInShiningArmani.'"

"What's wrong with that?"

"It's weird. He knows my name is Bianca, and I know his name is Matt, so why doesn't he use our real names? And, well, we've never met. It's too much too soon."

"He's trying to sweep you off your feet." Rosie sounded matter-of-fact.

"Well, listen to the e-mail he sent me last night. 'Dear CreativeGirlNYC, I was very disappointed that you canceled our date and now won't accept my calls. I've been waiting for us to meet for a long time. In fact, I've been counting down the days until I can make you mine. I feel that you are playing games with me, and I don't appreciate it. If you are willing to meet me tonight, let me know.'"

"Wow, he's persistent."

"Then today, he just sent me another e-mail. 'Answer me, Bianca. If you would like to meet for lunch we can still make it work. If not, it's your loss.'"

"Wow. He does sound like a winner, doesn't he?" Rosie exclaimed, and I nodded, though she couldn't see me.

"Now you know why I won't be dating online anymore." I closed my laptop.

"We'll find two hotties tonight and flirt the night away."

"Sounds good to me."

"You might finally get laid," she said, and then giggled.

"Rosie!"

"Hey, I'm just being honest. A vibrator can only do so much."

"I'll see you tonight," I groaned.

"HEY," ROSIE WHISPERED into the phone as I picked it up.

"Hey back at ya."

"Meet me at this new bar on the Upper West Side tonight. I've heard good things and want to check it out."

"What's it called?"

"Orange."

"Okay. I'll see you around six?"

"Yeah," she paused. "Six sounds good." Then she giggled, the noise sounded quite nervous and I frowned into the phone.

"What's so funny? Is there a reason why you chose this bar, Rosie?" My brain started ticking, and I took a gulp of water.

"I'll tell you later," she said hurriedly, and then hung up.

I CHECKED MY watch for the tenth time. It was now six forty-five and I was starting to get impatient. I looked at the menu again, and my stomach rumbled as I read the different entrée descriptions. I was so hungry, and I could already feel the glass of wine I was sipping, going to my head.

I texted Rosie a photo of the cute bartender and then rubbed my temple softly. Hopefully the surreptitious photo I'd taken would make her hurry up.

"Hey," Rosie walked into the bar as if she owned it, oblivious to the stares of the men in the bar as she sauntered towards me. Her blonde hair was perfectly coiffed and her Escada suit clung to her body perfectly.

"Hey," I jumped up and gave her a quick hug and continental kiss. Left cheek, right cheek, left cheek. "I just text you, by the way!"

I looked at her expensive suit enviously. "You're lucky I work from home or I'd be borrowing your clothes." I laughed as we sat down. I instinctively grabbed to the right of me to make sure the plastic bag was still at my side. I was going to give Rosie a copy my father's papers to hold for safekeeping. I'd taken the originals and put them in my safety deposit box at the bank, but I wanted to make sure that I had multiple copies out there just in case.

"How goes the writing? Seen any good movies lately?" She smiled at me briefly before turning to call the waiter over.

"Depends on what you mean by good?" I shrugged. "I've been watching Box Office movies mainly, those are the reviews that get the hits. Not the art pieces we used to watch in college."

"Good old action movies huh?"

"Action and cheesy romance." I smiled and picked up my glass of wine. "They all start to seem the same, but they pay well. I had an article on Channing Tatum get ten thousand views last week."

"Well, I'd pay to see him swinging those hips." Rosie frowned as she waited for someone to come over and take her order. "The service here sucks. I should have remembered from last time."

"Oh you've been here before?" I asked her curiously, I was pretty sure she had said this was her first time.

"Yeah, once." She ran her hands through her hair and then leaned towards me and grinned. "I've missed you, Bianca. I feel like we haven't seen each other in ages."

"That's because we haven't."

"I bought you something the other day." She studied my face and grinned. "A book on Richard III and the lost princes or whatever."

"Oh awesome." I leaned back in my chair. "You know that some men at the Tower of London recently found..."

"So you have to tell me all about that guy online." She interrupted me and then paused and turned around. "Waiter," she called out loudly. "Can you come over here when you have a chance. I'd like a drink sometime this year." She turned back to me with a glint in her eyes and a small smile. "Let's see how long he takes now."

"He's most probably busy, Rosie." I shook my head at her impatience. "You've only been here for a few minutes."

"Exactly, I've been here for a few minutes and I'm still sober." She shuddered. "Something is wrong with this picture."

"You can have some of my wine if you want?" I pointed to the bottle on the table and she shook her head.

"No, I think I'm going to get a cocktail." She said quickly. "I need liquor tonight."

"So how's work?" I changed the subject and inquired about her job. I really wanted to talk about myself, but I didn't want to be rude.

"Challenging." She shrugged. "We're attempting to get the account of one of the top financial companies in the States. I can't tell you the name, for legal reasons, but let's just say if we get it, we will be one of the top advisement companies in the world."

"Do you think you'll get it?"

"If I have anything to say about it, yes." She pursed her lips. "Of course I'm not working on that deal. I'm helping James with the Bradley Inc., deal. If we get that, I think I'll get promoted. That's why I've been so busy."

"Oh." I looked down into my glass of wine; my heart was racing at her words. I hadn't known she was trying to do business with the Bradley Corporation. "That's David's dad's company." I said casually, pretending that that fact was unimportant.

"Oh yeah, that's where I saw him a couple of weeks ago. In the offices." She made a face and I knew that she was worried that I was still upset that we had broken up. Rosie didn't know that I had never really had legitimate feelings for David, so his cheating hadn't really hurt me.

"I need to tell you something." I took a deep breath and lowered my voice. "It's about David and well the Bradley Company."

"Oh?" Her eyes narrowed and she looked at me in interest.

"What about them?"

"I think that the Bradley Company had something to do with what happened to my mother."

"What are you talking about?" She looked confused. "What happened to your mom? She died in a car crash, didn't she?"

"That's the thing." I took a deep breath, hoping Rosie wasn't going to think I was crazy. "I don't think she did."

"Oh?"

"Remember how my dad used to work as an inventor?" I rushed out. "Well, he used to work for the Bradley Company. In fact when the company was started it was called, Bradley, London, and Maxwell. I think..."

"Hold on a second." She jumped up quickly. "I just need to go to the restroom room okay?"

I noticed someone in the corner of the bar staring at me. He looked vaguely familiar, but I couldn't place him. I nodded at Rosie slowly as my head started to feel heavy. I was being watched. I was certain of it. I took a deep breath and looked around me. Was I being listened to as well? Part of me was glad that Rosie had jumped up when she had. Then it hit me; it was the man who'd been staring at me from behind the newspaper at the coffee shop.

"That's fine." I mumbled back, the words tripping out of mouth in an existential fashion. I wanted to jump up and run, but I knew that wouldn't help. I'd ask Rosie for her advice when she came back from the restroom. I'd tell her everything that was going on and then hope she wasn't angry at me for keeping it all from her for so long.

"Watch my bag for me." She handed me her large black Balenciaga bag and walked away quickly. I put her bag in my lap and quickly unzipped it and placed the plastic bag with the copies of my father's papers in it and did it back up again.

"More wine, mam?" I heard the voice in front of me and I felt a prick in my arm as I looked up. I didn't see the face of the person as I looked up because my vision became dotted. All of a sudden, I felt terribly drowsy, like I wanted to sleep. I closed my eyes for a second, and then the world went black.

The first time I regained consciousness, I could feel someone lifting me up. I tried to open my eyes to see what was going on, but my eyelids wouldn't open because they were too weak. The second time I regained consciousness, I could hear two men frantically whispering something. It sounded like, "The plan's changed. The plan's changed."

I opened my mouth to speak, but nothing came out. I allowed the dark void to suck me back in as my brain realized that the inevitable had happened. I knew that I'd rather be unconscious than frozen in fear while being blind and speechless. The void was good for now. The void would allow to me to conserve my energy and stop the panic that was currently running through my body.

I drifted back into oblivion, and all I could think about were David's words the last time we'd spoken. *You're strong, Bianca. You can handle anything. I promise that you'll get over this.* I only hoped that I was as strong as he thought I was.

CPSIA information can be obtained
at www.ICGtesting.com
Printed in the USA
LVOW13s1520280118
564334LV00012B/840/P